"Why did you make love to me, then act as though you regretted it?"

Jon wasn't prepared for a showdown with Tracy. "Your emotions are wired, and you feel as if you're in danger. That can ruin your judgment."

"In other words, I want you because of some wacky emotional response to the danger I'm in. Do you have any idea what that makes me sound like? Or you? I thought you offered me honesty. My mistake."

Jon stared at her, watching the life flow out of her eyes, seeing an emptiness that touched him all the way to his soul.

"My profession is hell on marriages and relationships," he said quietly. "I won't put anyone I care about through that kind of torture. You have courage and compassion. You belong with a man who can give you a beautiful life. I can't."

Dear Reader,

When two people fall in love, the world is suddenly new and exciting, and it's that same excitement we bring to you in Silhouette Intimate Moments. These are stories with scope and grandeur. The characters lead lives we all dream of, and everything they do reflects the wonder of being in love.

Longer and more sensuous than most romances, Silhouette Intimate Moments novels take you away from everyday life and let you share the magic of love. Adventure, glamour, drama, even suspense—these are the passwords that let you into a world where love has a power beyond the ordinary, where the best authors in the field today create stories of love and commitment that will stay with you always.

In coming months look for novels by your favorite authors: Kathleen Creighton, Heather Graham Pozzessere, Nora Roberts and Marilyn Pappano, to name just a few. And whenever you buy books, look for all the Silhouette Intimate Moments, love stories *for* today's woman *by* today's woman.

Leslie J. Wainger
Senior Editor
Silhouette Books

Sara Chance
Fire in the Night

Silhouette Intimate Moments

Published by Silhouette Books New York

America's Publisher of Contemporary Romance

SILHOUETTE BOOKS
300 East 42nd St., New York, N.Y. 10017

ISBN: 0-373-07299-6

First Silhouette Books printing August 1989

All the characters in this book are fictitious. Any
resemblance to actual persons, living or dead, is
purely coincidental.

®: Trademark used under license and
registered in the United States Patent and
Trademark Office and in other countries.

Printed in the U.S.A.

SARA CHANCE

lives on Florida's Gold Coast. Asked why she writes romance, she replies, "I live it and believe in it. After all, I met and married my husband, David, in less than six weeks." That was two teenage daughters and twenty years ago. Two of Sara's Desires, *Her Golden Eyes* and *A Touch of Passion*, were nominated by *Romantic Times* in the Best Desire category for their publishing years. And *Double Solitaire* was a Romance Writers of America Golden Medallion nominee.

Chance provides all kinds of opportunities for those who care to look. An invitation to do a call-in radio talk show one Sunday morning gave me a glimpse into a media world I had taken for granted. This story is my attempt at a word picture of the skill, dedication and intelligence of the men and women I met and liked at WJNO radio. Thank you John, Mike and Roger for answering all my questions with such patience. Especially thank you, Wendy, for allowing me to follow you around for a day to collect the feelings I needed for Tracy. I hope you like the result.

And finally, thank you Henry Marshall for your invaluable help about the firebug, his methods and the methods of those who sought to catch him.

Prologue

The building stood silent, empty on the wide down-town street. Tomorrow it would have been filled to capacity with workers and those doing business within its pale pink stucco walls. But this was its last moment to rise against the south Florida skyline. Two hundred yards away, a shadow moved stealthily through the gloom. No sound marred the stillness. Three a.m. was the deepest part of the night in this section of the city.

The man whom the newspapers had dubbed the firebug took a deep breath. The most risky part of the operation was over. Once again he had succeeded in temporarily circumventing a building's fire and burglar alarms. Anticipation built in him for that moment when the crude but effective timers he had set on each of the structure's three floors would go off. Small explosions would ignite the gas and diesel fuel mixture, setting alight the blazes that would ultimately connect to eat Lightning Graphics alive. Three minutes later another charge set on the roof would explode, blowing a hole up top that would create a concrete chimney out of the building. The greedy flames, needing oxygen to survive, would claw at the walls, racing for the sky. And he would see it all, just as he had seen it all before and would again before he was done.

Three years. Long months of work, watching, moving from one job to another and planning. He glanced at his watch, starting the countdown.

Five. Four. Three. Two. *One!*

The simultaneous explosions rocked the street. He estimated ten minutes, maximum, before the fire department would arrive. As he waited, he saw the first fingers of fire from the deadly orange beast he had begun to love.

A windowpane shattered, spitting splinters into the air, lethal missiles that had as yet hurt no one. He frowned, angry that he had been unable to find a way to eliminate this risk. He was no killer. But those he sought to punish were. He destroyed. But he did not kill.

With a loud explosion from the roof, the operation was complete. Soon, no one would be able to stop what he had done this night. The fire was alive now, beyond control. The heat reached him, moving delicately over his skin like a lover's caress. He smiled, feeling the power of his accomplishment surge through him.

Fire sirens wailed, screaming useless protests. He melted deeper into the shadows, preparing to leave. To stay was to risk detection before his mission was complete. Soon, he would be done. But not tonight.

Chapter 1

This just in from our WDRU news department on the scene. The firebug has hit again. This time, Lightning Graphics was the target. Firemen did their best, but by the time they arrived the building was too far gone for them to do more than control the blaze and save the structures on either side. The state fire marshal's office, when contacted by our reporter, announced that they are continuing to investigate what appears to be a serial firebug in our city. When pressed they admitted that the only leads they have concern the method rather than the perpetrator. Stay tuned for developments.''

Tracy Michaels looked up from the newspaper she was scanning to listen to the morning radio report. The speakers tucked into the corners of the large room that was one big office for eight WDRU hosts and producers were tuned to the station. She frowned on hearing the details.

"Do you think that guy heard your program on the firebug yesterday and decided to give the public another taste of his talent?" Nikki, Tracy's best friend, asked as she also paused to listen.

"I hope not. That guy is running rings around the fire marshal's office. You heard the calls yesterday. The public is poised between curiosity and anger. They want action and aren't getting it. The business sector is starting to put pressure on the mayor."

"And we know how much pressure *that* is."

"It's going to be even worse now." Tracy leaned back in her chair, the task of cutting and pasting articles from today's news that would be of interest to her audience no longer holding first place in her attention.

"What do you mean?"

"Remember that show I did on the involvement of town officials in small businesses last month?" At Nikki's nod she continued. "Don't you remember that the mayor and his brother own Lightning Graphics? Of course the mayor stays behind the scenes for the most part. That fact got quite a number of calls, if memory serves, especially when it turned out that LG does most of the outside work for the city. This latest spotlight on their business won't make the mayor's day."

"I'd forgotten that. Your memory and your ability to dig up facts are incredible. You've been in this town a little more than four months and you have information that I don't know, and I've lived here most of my life."

Tracy's green eyes twinkled at Nikki's disgruntled tone. She laughed softly. "I can't take credit for the first, but the second is easy. I'm just naturally nosy. Coming from a small town gave me a taste for knowing everything about everybody."

"Fiddle," Nikki grumbled, picking up one of the newsmagazines she was perusing. "What you mean is that you look as if butter wouldn't melt in your mouth and people tell you things. I never saw anyone who had more of a capacity for worming information out of the most determined human clam. I get down on my knees every day and thank heaven you aren't the ruthless type who believes in crawling over people to get ahead professionally."

Tracy wasn't sure whether to feel complimented or insulted at Nikki's description. It was true she didn't want to succeed at someone's expense, but it wasn't true that she wasn't ambitious. She just had different ways of going about getting what she wanted. She had always believed in finesse over brawn.

Tracy returned to her research while continuing the conversation. One thing her job had taught her was how to do many things at once. Some might think radio a dying medium but they were wrong. It was as alive and as hectic and demanding a profession as any of its more publicized relatives.

"You make me sound like a marshmallow."

"And Mount Saint Helens is just a mountain," Nikki grunted as she answered her phone.

Tracy smiled at the analogy. Without knowing it, Nikki had touched a chord, not in Tracy's professional life but in her personal one. There had been a time when she was first cousin to the erupting volcano. Lee had felt the hot flow of lava in her anger. She had been tried many times in her life, but never so sorely as when she had discovered that she had made love with a married man. The pain of his lies and betrayal had shown her all her own strengths and weaknesses. Now, a few months past her twenty-ninth birthday, Tracy had made peace with herself. She was no longer naive, no longer trusting and certainly no longer unscarred by the harsh realities of life, but she was no longer running, either. West Palm Beach was a new home, a new area and a new beginning. Whatever mistakes she had made in Virginia would remain there. Today was what mattered.

The man smiled as he listened to the radio, and popped the top of the soft drink in his hand. He was outwitting those who would catch him. The first few fires had left him worried about getting caught before he could finish. Now, he knew differently. With each job he had learned how to work faster and cleaner. He was no longer concerned about being apprehended.

Satisfied with his night's work, he relaxed with his favorite station, WDRU. The small efficiency apartment didn't come equipped with a television, but he didn't mind. Between his job and his nighttime activities he didn't have many free moments. Besides, WDRU beat the newspapers and television with its reporting. And it also had Tracy Michaels. His favorite radio personality wasn't on the air until the morning, but right now, if he paid attention to the breaks between the programs, he sometimes could hear her doing a commercial.

* * *

"Jon, Sam wants to see you when you get finished with that report." Roger dropped into his chair with a groan and tried another swallow of coffee to help him wake up.

Around the two men, the room was cluttered. Other detectives were sitting at littered desks, writing reports, discussing strategy or talking on the phone. The smells and sounds were universal to such places. A sense of urgency and purpose formed an underlying rhythm to every movement.

Jon Kent looked up from the police report he was typing, and sized up Roger's condition with a glance. "You should be at home with that cold. We've earned the time off."

"Yeah, isn't it the truth. Six weeks on that con sting without a break. It's a wonder I'm still vertical after spending two of those weeks in the rain. Why couldn't we have a drought like the rest of the country?"

Jon ignored the rhetorical question to finish the job at hand. Where Roger tended to be flash and brilliance, sometimes missing important subtleties in his race for the truth, Jon was a steady, driving force that could be neither turned nor deflected from his course once set. Even in looks the two differed greatly. Roger was lean with an intensity that drew the eye. Jon was a big man who moved with lazy grace through a world seen through sleepy black eyes that never showed shock or surprise. And yet, for all Roger's glitz, when the going got tough he could not match Jon in speed or quick thinking. Jon had been alternately described as a loner, complex, brilliant—and he was impossible to read, even for his friend and partner of eight years.

Roger watched Jon type for a moment, then finished his coffee. "Give me that damn report and you go see what Sam wants. It's my turn to do the thing, anyway."

Jon corrected his last mistake and pulled the paper from the typewriter. "Your timing is, as always, uncanny. I'm finished." He tossed the sheet across the surface of the two desks facing each other. "Sign it and you're done."

"I owe you one, buddy," Roger murmured, barely glancing at the detailed account of his part in the last assignment. He didn't need to check the work to know it was letter-perfect. Jon made few mistakes and those he did he caught.

Jon collected his coat from the back of the chair, shrugging into it as he walked. Sam's office was down the hall from the main detective room. He responded absently to the few greetings of those he passed, his mind already sifting through the possible reasons for the summons to the chief's office.

Jon knocked on the door, waiting for the growled response before entering. Sam had his sleeves rolled to his elbows, an unlit cigarette dangling from his lips and a scowl on his face. All three signs were harbingers of bad news. Jon sighed deeply as he took a chair.

Sam glared at him for a long moment. "You give me a pain, Kent. The rest of my staff, with the exception of that partner of yours, would be curious about why I called you in here. You just sit there looking half-asleep."

"You should be used to me by now." Jon's voice rumbled slowly from a chest that a weight lifter would happily have laid claim to. "I'll humor you if it makes you happy. What's up?"

"My tail and yours," Sam replied, spitting the words out. "I've just had a call from the mayor. That damn torch set fire to his business last night. He's hopping mad and ready to string up everybody in the fire marshal's office by their thumbs for not stopping this creep. He wants action and he wants us to give it to him. On top of that, he's got some lunatic idea that some crazy broad over at WDRU might know something about the firebug. It seems his secretary is a fan of this Tracy Michaels female and listens to her show while working. Ms. Michaels did a show on the firebug and got some interesting calls that the mayor's secretary thought sounded odd."

Jon's interest was piqued at the mention of Tracy's name. He had caught her call-in talk show a few times since she had come to WDRU. He'd been impressed with her warmth and incisive handling of tricky issues. Intelligence in any form always intrigued him.

"One call, especially, lit a fire under the mayor. Some weirdo called in yesterday and hinted at a fire being scheduled for last night. As far I'm concerned I'd just as soon leave this whole mess in the fire department's hands—we've got bigger game to catch. But the mayor isn't going to lay off. According to him the fire people haven't much to go on beyond the methods of arson. The report of their findings is being sent over sometime today. I'll give it to you as soon as it arrives, since you and Roger are, as of this moment, officially on the assignment."

"Roger won't thank you for this case. You know he likes the danger type stuff," Jon said as he got to his feet.

Sam grinned, his eyes alight with satisfaction. "Good. Since I'm being hounded to death by politicians and irritated department heads, I think I'll spread a little of my misery his way." He chomped on his cigarette, biting it in two, then swore as he waved Jon out.

Jon concealed a grin as he returned to his desk. Roger and Sam had had a polite feud going since Roger's rookie days. Neither man showed any signs of remembering its cause but wasn't about to yell cease-fire. And he was in the middle, often acting as referee when one got hold of a really good stinger for the other.

"Don't tell me what he wanted. I don't want to know." Roger pulled himself to his feet when Jon made no effort to sit down.

"It's not so bad." Jon chuckled at Roger's disbelieving look. "We're going to see Tracy Michaels."

"I'm not up to crossing the t's and dotting the i's this morning. Just give it to me straight. What does the darling of the early-morning public forum have to do with us?"

"I'll tell you while I drive us to WDRU."

"I hate it when you drive. I wish I had never agreed to splitting the honors. You drive like an old lady," Roger grumbled, following Jon out of the room.

"No, you drive like a race driver with a death wish," Jon returned with a grin. "I want to get there alive."

Tracy finished cutting out the last of the news articles she had chosen from the papers. Keeping aware of timely topics was a never-ending job but one that was necessary. She glanced at the clock on the wall. Five minutes to air. Feeling the energy build up within, she smiled a little to herself. She had never gotten over the thrill of facing a mike with nothing more than her mind and her ability to interact with her listeners. Rising, she collected the pertinent material for today's show on the hotly disputed bond issue.

"Ready, Nikki?" she asked as she neared Nikki's desk.

"Yeah, I can finish my research while I take care of the phone lines for you. My visit from that blasted commissioner put me behind schedule this morning."

"Wait until you get her beside you at the mike," Tracy warned as they entered the small control room. Both women had their own shows and screened the incoming calls for the other. "How's it going, Walter?" Tracy asked in greeting to her program's technical director.

"Like silk." He didn't pause in his job, his eyes remaining glued to the huge panel of knobs and dials before him. He cued the male host who was on just before Tracy, then punched the taped news segment that ran between the two shows.

Tracy exchanged a short word with her co-worker as she replaced him in front of the mike. Putting on the headset that allowed her to hear the calls that were fed into the room, she readjusted the height of the mike then nodded her readiness to Walter.

In the control room, Nikki took her place in the chair in front of a computer that linked the phone lines with the small monitor before Tracy. The five lines were numbered on each screen, so that Nikki could type in the first name, the city of origin and the subject addressed by each caller. The person manning the phones helped to keep up the pace of the show by juggling various points of view for maximum audience appeal. Tracy glanced at Walter, waiting and listening to the last of the network news. He gave her the cue as her theme music began.

"Good morning, this is Tracy Michaels on the air with this morning's edition of the *Tracy Michaels Show....*"

"Will you listen to that guy? Damn fool, making a spectacle of himself." Roger slumped in his seat. "I hate talk shows."

"Shut up, Roger." Jon Kent guided their unmarked car through the streets, listening closely to the expert way Tracy Michaels handled a potentially explosive caller. The woman had style and courage. No matter how abusive any of her callers got, she kept her temper and her sense of humor.

Roger sneezed, cursed, then sneezed again. "This is not turning into a good day," he muttered irritably. "I think the mayor is really reaching on this one. What could a little-known radio personality from a town in Virginia know about the firebug?"

Jon glanced at his partner, amused at the vehemence in his voice. "That cold is making you even more obnoxious than usual," he shot back, chuckling. "Where did you get that part about Virginia, anyway?"

"Out of the newspaper. They did an article on her when she first came to town. Her picture was kind of pretty. Lots of dark hair around an attractive face. Not bad but not my style." Roger leaned back in his seat with a deep, congested sigh. "I feel like I've been run over by a truck."

Jon returned his attention to the radio. The tone of the show had changed, slowed, mellowed into a real exchange of information from both men and woman. Jon listened, becoming more intrigued and curious. Now that Roger had pointed out Tracy's roots he could hear the faint Southern accent. The sound was soothing, strangely at odds with the sharp mind he had sensed in her handling of her show. He always had had an appreciation of complexities, of multidimensional situations and puzzles. Tracy's part in their investigation and the woman herself were pieces that as yet had no place in the whole picture. He turned into the small parking lot that served WDRU.

The station fronted on Lake Worth, a wide part of the intracoastal, the saltwater channel that ran the length of the state, providing a water highway for the marine population. The view was pure Florida: palm trees, sun-gilded water, white yachts moored in front of the Palm Beach mansions on the opposite shore. Jon noted the setting without paying any special attention to it.

"You want to do this interview or shall I?" Roger asked as they entered the lobby and gave their names and stated their business to a blond woman sitting behind the desk.

"Dumb question, Landis. When do I ever want to do the talking? That's your talent, not mine. Unless your cold isn't up to it."

Roger shrugged. "I'll survive."

Both men turned as the receptionist said, "Mr. Lynch will see you now. Ms. Michaels is still on the air. She has about twenty minutes left," she added gesturing them to follow her.

Roger perked up at the interested look she gave him. Jon saw the masculine gleam of approval in his eyes and stirred restlessly. Roger was a flirt whom women, no matter what age, couldn't seem to resist. At the moment Jon would have handed over a month's pay to share Roger's lighthearted approach to relationships. He had been burned badly once, losing the woman he'd loved. His job and his commitment to it had cost him more than he had thought he could pay. But pay he had and now he possessed the scars to prove the cost.

"Right here, gentlemen." The blonde knocked once then stepped back. Her smile was admiring as Roger walked by.

Jon ignored the interplay, as the door opened and he confronted the manager of the station. Jasper Lynch was well into his fifties but lean and trim with the age. The shrewd look in his eyes and his firm handshake said no nonsense would be tolerated in his domain. Jon respected the man on sight.

"To what do I owe the pleasure of this visit?" Jasper asked, taking a seat behind his desk.

Jon pulled out his notebook while Roger settled in his chair. He was the note taker and Roger the interrogator.

"We have a bit of a problem and we're hoping you could help us. It concerns the *Tracy Michaels Show* and the segment on the firebug that was done yesterday. As of this morning my partner and I have been assigned to help in the firebug investigation. The mayor wants this thing settled, pronto. We hope your Ms. Michaels may be able to help us."

Jasper divided his attention between both men, his gaze lingering longer on Jon before he replied to Roger's comment. "How can we help? It was an ordinary show. Nothing specifically out of the way," Jasper pointed out.

"There was one thing. According to one of our sources, there was a guy at the end of the show who had a rather unusual point of view about the firebug."

"We get a few of those occasionally. As I'm sure you know it's usually just someone wanting attention." Jasper shrugged, his eyes sharp.

Roger sighed resignedly. "I read somewhere that sometimes shows like this use special people to kind of help a controversy along."

Jasper's look narrowed. "You mean a plant? Someone I or one of my people set up to make the show look good?"

"It has happened," Jon murmured quietly.

"Not here it hasn't, and won't. We don't do that kind of stuff. Don't need to, especially with a show as popular as Tracy's."

Roger spread his hands apologetically. "We had to ask. As I'm sure you know, the investigation isn't going as quickly as we would like."

"I assume you tape your shows for the records," Jon said.

"Always."

"We'd like to hear the last—" He broke off what he was saying to listen to Tracy's final caller of the day. Tracy's show was playing softly in the background.

"Yes, Bo, I remember you from yesterday," Tracy replied. "Do you have something for us on the bond issue?"

"No. I wanted to know what you think of this last fire set by the firebug?"

Tracy hesitated, glanced through the glass at the clock hanging on the control room wall. Nikki caught her eye, shrugged and looked puzzled.

"I haven't formed an opinion yet, but that isn't the issue today."

"I thought you would be wondering what he plans to do next."

Tracy sighed, annoyed the man wouldn't take the hint. It was almost time to close the show. "I think we're all wondering about that, but we really don't have time to go into the problem today. The clock tells me I have to say goodbye until tomorrow. Hope all your problems are little ones and all your successes great. This is Tracy Michaels for the *Tracy Michaels*

Show." Pulling off her headset, Tracy got out of her chair just as Nikki came into the room.

"I'm sorry. That guy told me he wanted to discuss the bond issue."

Tracy frowned, thinking the caller's not specifying his question when talking to Nikki was one thing, outright lying quite another. "Callers like that always make me a little edgy. I hope that's the last we hear of him for a while."

"I know the feeling. He's distorting his voice so badly that it's immediately noticeable on the phone, and he's lying to get on a show that has nothing to do with what he wants to talk about. Do you suppose he *is* the firebug?"

Tracy shifted her shoulders. "I don't know. I wouldn't think so. According to the papers the firebug hasn't made any mistakes so far. It isn't logical for him to come out of hiding just to talk to me or to get on the air with a lot of vague chat."

Walter poked his head around the door. "The boss wants to see you. Hear he's got two detectives with him. What have you been up to, Tracy?" He grinned as he ducked back around the corner before Tracy could answer.

Tracy's brow furrowed at the news. "How much you want to bet it's about this creep?"

Nikki spread her hands, shaking her head. "Not me. Your instincts are usually sounder than mine." She followed Tracy halfway to Jasper's office. "Yell if you need help."

Jon stared at the notebook in his hand. He hadn't placed much credence on coming over here. He had thought, as the chief thought, they were chasing a wild goose. Now he wasn't so certain. He didn't like the sound of Bo at all. He leaned back in his chair, waiting silently for Tracy to arrive.

A moment later the door opened gently and she was there. He turned his head to watch her walk the few feet from the entrance to a chair slightly angled off to one side of his. Roger was wrong, he realized. Tracy Michaels wasn't pretty, she was stunning, with the kind of body that gave a man ideas that could get him arrested even in this permissive era. Her eyes were green, clear, bright and intelligent. She moved with the grace of a dancer, and when she spoke he knew he'd remember her voice forever. Desire, unwelcome and definitely unexpected, stirred to life. The knowledge that the distance he had purposely built between himself and the world was being strained by a woman he had yet to be introduced to was a shock he could have done without. Things like this didn't happen to him. His life was founded on control, on mental and physical power, on focusing his emotions on the job at hand rather than on a useless release that might make him feel better but solved no problem.

As Jasper made the introductions, Tracy studied the two detectives openly. The first, Detective Roger Landis, was near six feet, lean, dark and dangerous looking. The second, Jon Kent, was a direct contrast to his partner, with shaggy light brown hair and a muscled frame that had to be around six feet three. His face was smooth, making him appear younger than Landis, with a more placid temperament than his counterpart's intense personality. His movements were slow, easy, as though he had all the time in the world to get from point A to point B.

"Ms. Michaels, we need to ask you a few questions." Tracy started at the clipped intrusion of Roger's voice.

She glanced at the detective, oddly surprised at how hard it was to pull her gaze from Jon Kent. She shook off the feeling, annoyed at herself for being distracted. One did not get called before two detectives for no reason.

"What kind of questions?" she asked warily, looking at Jasper for a clue. His expression betrayed nothing.

"We'd like you to tell us about one of your callers. The one who identifies himself as Bo."

Tracy frowned. So her intuition hadn't let her down. "There isn't much to tell. I heard from him for the first time yesterday and then he called back today. He isn't a regular, and both Nikki and I think he's disguising his voice."

Roger shot Jasper a look before saying, "I've already asked your boss this question, and now I need an answer from you. Is the man a plant? Maybe someone you've coached to lead into the next show or to stir up audience interest?"

Tracy stiffened at the suggestion, anger flashing in her eyes. "I do not *do* plants. I don't need to." She turned to Jasper. "Did you know about this?" Her anger increased a notch at Jasper's nod.

"He had the same reaction as you," Roger added.

Tracy's temper surprised Jon. He didn't like surprises. The lady looked cool and controlled, but there was a fire under that calm exterior. Jon closed his notebook and tucked it in his pocket. Spreading his hands when Tracy focused blazing eyes in his direction, he said, "It's our job to ask uncomfortable questions. We don't always agree but we do follow through. You should understand that."

"Usually when I ask questions like that one, I make sure there is some basis for the remark," she returned smartly. His voice was soothing, gentle. Without wanting to she found herself calming under its influence.

Roger shifted in his seat, stifling the urge to sneeze. "The point is, we've been brought into this situation blind. Until now there haven't been any real leads beyond the method of fire setting. Now this Bo character shows up. We have to be suspicious."

Tracy nodded, not liking the abrupt way Landis went after his information. Sharp men, ones who tended to steamroller, were not males she tolerated well. Her past had taught her not to trust the type. "I can understand that, but to set your minds at rest, I know nothing beyond what I've told you."

"Your boss has told us that you have tapes of the shows."

Tracy felt as if she were caught in the middle of a tennis match. First one man would say something and then the other. This time it was Jon. At least his remarks weren't borderline accusations. "So?"

"Would you have time to let us listen to the last two shows? Perhaps between the three of us, we might pick up something important?"

"She'll make time," Jasper answered before Tracy could.

Irritated at being railroaded into the situation when she would have agreed on her own, Tracy inhaled sharply. She noted that only Jon acted as though he sought her compliance. She nodded her agreement, intrigued that, of the three, he was the one watching her as a person rather than an employee or source of information. It was then she knew she was in trouble.

Jon smiled slightly. Until this moment his eyes had been half-closed. Now his lashes lifted to reveal the most mesmerizing black eyes she had ever seen. And she had thought *Roger* the more dangerous of the two. Error! Inadequate input! Had she been a computer the warning message would have been flashing across her screen.

Jon and Roger entered the station house after having spent the better part of the day listening to tapes of Tracy's shows. None of them had found anything.

One of the detectives looked up as they headed for their desks and said, "Sam wants to see you, Kent."

"This is where I came in," Roger muttered. "The shift is almost over. I think I'll head home, take a couple of cold tablets and call it a day. I can't handle Sam and the flu at the same time."

"Good idea. You look like a plate of cold eggs," Jon agreed, pausing only long enough to shrug out of his jacket and sling it over the back of his chair.

Roger grimaced at the description but didn't dispute it. "Make my excuses to our leader," he said as Jon headed for Sam's office.

Jon barely made it inside before Sam pounced.

"Well, what did you and that partner of yours get?" Sam settled in his chair as though he planned on taking root.

Jon leaned back, watching his former partner from his rookie days. "That sounds fairly desperate. Not like you. What's up now?"

"The mayor was back on the phone about an hour after you left. This time *he* was listening to that Michaels broadcast. He didn't like that Bo character, and he's madder than a wet cat that the guy's running loose while he's fighting with the insurance people about his losses. He wants action yesterday. The fire marshal is on my back about us being on the case—his pride is smarting. And we've got bigger fish to fry than this mess, anyway. If I had my way I'd forget the whole thing but I can't. So tell me you can get the mayor off my back and solve this thing."

This wasn't the first time Jon had gotten so many words tossed at him. His specialty was putting together puzzles or unraveling crimes. Without conceit he knew he was good; he worked at being better. Roger had the flash and flair, but he had the ability to sift through seemingly meaningless bits and pieces of a case and come up with solutions.

"Why is the whole town hopping after only three fires?"

"The fire marshal's office has connected them with similar problems in Orlando and Jacksonville. This guy blows into town, torches at will and then calmly walks out without anyone getting a decent shot at catching him. People in Orlando are practically foaming at the mouth over the eight fires he left as

mementos of his visit. Jacksonville's people remind me
of rabid dogs at the moment.''

"You've talked to them?" Jon's brows rose slightly
at the news.

"I didn't call them. They called me," Sam snapped
irritably. "I got an earful—in spades. Everyone wants
this guy's rear in a sling ASAP. Take what you need,
do whatever you have to do, but get this guy. Follow
this Tracy Michaels around, sit on her doorstep if
that's what it takes to get this case solved. Right now
she's our only lead." He handed Jon the folder that
had been lying on his desk. "Here's every piece of information we've got. Orlando and Jacksonville are
sending their stuff down to us today."

Jon scanned the papers in the folder quickly. "I
think we may need a tap-and-trace on her phone in the
near future, assuming of course this Bo character isn't
some nut looking for attention by pretending to know
something."

"I'll take care of that as soon as you give me enough
reason to go for it. Anything else?"

"No." Jon rose, tucked the folder under his arm,
his mind already busy sorting and sifting through the
small collection of facts.

"Then get out of my office so I can get some work
done."

Jon hardly heard the gruff command. He was
thinking of Tracy, wondering just how and why she
had come into the firebug picture. Was her choice of
programming that one day the link, or was there
more? And what was he going to do about his in-
creasing interest in the woman herself? Sitting with her
in that small room while they had reviewed the tapes

had been a subtle kind of torture. Her perfume had been as light as a spring breeze, and he could still feel the way his senses had responded. He had known every movement she made. Her attitude had alternated between bad temper and honest attempts at helpfulness. Roger had prodded her, trying to get more information any way possible, while he himself had sat back to watch and listen. And feel. Too much.

Seeing her, talking with her, had not brought an end to his curiosity. He didn't like being drawn to her. He didn't want to get close to her or any woman. And most of all he didn't want to discover that the control he had developed for so long was suddenly an effort to maintain.

He had to remember Amanda and the lessons she had taught him. But even that was an effort at the moment. All he could recall was a pair of vivid green eyes blazing with temper and insulted professional pride.

Chapter 2

Bye, Tracy, thanks for the ride home. With any kind of luck the garage will have my car ready this evening." Nikki slid out of the car, giving Tracy a smile before heading up the walk to the condo complex.

Tracy gave her friend a wave and watched for an opening in the rush-hour traffic. Even after four months it still took all her concentration to make the drive from the downtown radio station to her home in Jupiter, some fifteen miles to the north. Finding a small slot in the stream of cars, she grinned and shot away from the curb. Tomorrow she would hear about her racetrack-style driving from Nikki, but the price was worth the reward of getting home quicker.

It had been a long, eventful day. The image of Jon Kent slipped into her mind. He had been interfering with her thought processes since the moment she met him, and she couldn't figure out why. His partner was the type most women would find attractive. Why did she have to be the exception, caught by a lazy air and a pair of black eyes that looked as though they could see into her soul?

She wasn't ready for a man in her life. Getting back on track after Lee had been difficult and at times almost more than she could handle. Peace and a sense of order were finally more than just a dream to Tracy, and she wanted to keep things that way. In due time she would reenter the dating game and hopefully get herself someone nice and settled, someone she could trust and depend on to love and be loved by. She did not want some deceptively sexy male with a shaggy mop of brown hair and a smile that could make her believe every day would be Christmas unraveling all her plans.

Suddenly Tracy felt very confined. She switched off the air-conditioning in the car and rolled down the windows. Instantly she felt freer, released from the artificial environment of the temperature-controlled atmosphere. Tracy decided to just do her job, cooperate with the police over her caller and stay out of Jon Kent's way until the situation that had thrown them together resolved itself. Satisfied, she settled back to enjoy what was left of the drive home.

Tracy turned up the volume of the radio and tuned in to a competitor station with a hot brand of rock music. She sang as she drove. Twenty minutes later she pulled into her drive, which was sheltered by a tangled mass of trees sadly in need of trimming. The air was marginally cooler in the shade, allowing her to take a moment to admire the home she was fashioning out of the fixer-upper that the real estate agent hadn't believed she intended to buy just for herself.

Two stories of old Florida construction peeked out of a lush, untamed jungle. There was a stone walkway somewhere under the debris littering what eventually would be her front yard. She knew because she had found it just this morning, to the ruin of her best pair of shoes. The inside of the house had been just as uncared for as the exterior, hardly a prospect to encourage anyone to buy the three-bedroom, two-bath structure despite the low asking price. What had sold Tracy was the waterway that formed the south border of her backyard. With this part of the Loxahatchee River too shallow for boating enthusiasts and too inaccessible for fishermen, her little house was a perfect hideaway right in the oldest section of town. With a check, a prayer, a home repair manual and a lot of sweat she was beginning to resurrect her derelict.

Smiling a little at the impression her home gave visitors, Tracy got out of the car and carefully negotiated the walk. This time she had no intention of taking a header on those bricks. Right after supper she was getting in her work clothes and finding every one of the little fiends if it took all night. Tracy climbed the three steps to the front porch and unlocked the door. The scratch of claws on the newly polished wood floors warned her Handsome was on his way to greet her.

"Hello, Handsome," she said as the dog glided into view. "I've got your food." She shook the giant bag she held as proof, laughing as the huge animal lifted his head and brushed his nose against her neck. He never was so sloppy as to lick her.

Handsome was nothing like his name. If there was a breed unrepresented in his ancestry, the American Kennel Club had never heard of it. The expression "it's so ugly it has to be cute" would never apply in his case. He was so ugly he was still ugly. Long legs, probably Great Dane, ended in huge feet. Shaggy, coarse hair, a mixture of every color known in dogdom, covered a lean body. His head was more wolf-like than dog, and his golden eyes watched everything and everyone with a degree of concentration usually given to humankind.

Tracy shifted her burden onto his broad back before heading down the hall to the kitchen. Handsome followed closely at her heels. Sunlight streamed in the windows that faced the water, creating prisms of color around the white, lime-green and candy-apple-red room. This had been her first project, the adage "do the worst first" her motto. White appliances, a natural brick floor, wood counters and green latticework wallpaper were set off by the apple stencil border around every window and door.

"What shall I have for dinner tonight, my friend?" Living alone had given Tracy the habit of talking to her pet as though he were human.

"I'm beginning to feel like a frozen dinner. But with the chores I still have waiting for me, I don't have time to cook for real." She stared at the well-stocked freezer section and sighed deeply as she pulled a package of lasagna from the stack of cartons. Popping the contents in the microwave she turned to the patiently waiting Handsome and pulled the sack from his shoulders, carrying it into the walk-in pantry.

While dinner was heating she went upstairs to change into her work clothes. The summer days were long, so she could put the extra hours to good use. Besides, she liked working with her hands, finding the activity relaxing after the mental demands of her job. She glanced around the bedroom on her way out, pleased with the cream-and-rust color scheme she had chosen. She was almost done with the inside of the house, having only the third bedroom remaining. It had taken her three months of working every weekend and most evenings to get this far. Nikki thought Tracy was crazy to devote so many hours to her home while neglecting her personal life. Tracy had tried explaining, but Nikki still hadn't understood why having a settled environment was so important to her.

Maybe no one could understand what it did to a person to discover that her life was built around a tissue of lies. Maybe no one would understand her need to control rather than be controlled by her environment and circumstances. Not that it mattered now. These days there was no one to please but herself.

Tracy smiled slightly at her own idiosyncrasies and left the room. Soon she would have her place in shape, then she would start accepting one or two of the invitations that had come her way in the past few months. She didn't need to think to know she was lonely. She had been lonely in Virginia, too. The selection of datable men hadn't been all that wide. She had met only one special man. For three years she had been everything a wife could be to Lee, encouraging, consoling, his lover and, she thought, his friend. She'd been a fool! The pain was no longer crippling, but it was still there hiding in the dark corners of her soul. Lee had used her, betrayed her trust and her love. How could she have known he was married, not just married but a father as well? To her dying day she would never forget the knock on the door that Thursday morning. The sight of his wife, a slight, untidily dressed woman in her late thirties, standing awkwardly on her porch while rain turned the world gray around them, was one she could not banish from her mind.

The truth had come out in a rush of words, tearing Tracy's world apart and leaving her adrift in a sea of rage, pain and broken promises. Picking up the pieces had taken nearly all her strength. But she had done it, pulling up stakes and taking a new job in a new city.

Tracy pushed away from the wall and shook off the memories. When she got involved with a man again she would make sure it was someone she could trust with her life. She wasn't looking for flash or glitz. Liking fast cars was her only vice. She didn't want a fast man. Staying power, strength, security and honesty were the qualities she would search for, and this time she wouldn't leap into a relationship based on little more than attraction. She wanted no more surprises on her doorstep.

"Yeah, what is it?" Jon grunted as he rolled over, the phone pressed to his ear. He peered at the clock on the nightstand. It had been past midnight before he'd been able to fall asleep. Now it was just after four and he wasn't in a good mood.

"The firebug hit again."

Jon came alert swiftly, recognizing the voice on the phone as one of the detectives on the night shift.

"That's impossible. The man doesn't take out two places in less than three nights. Are you sure?"

"As sure as we can be at this point. Same M.O. The building went up like a Roman candle. No injuries and a hole in the roof."

Jon pushed himself upright. "Does Sam know yet?"

"Yeah, and the mayor."

Jon cursed under his breath. He wouldn't get any more sleep tonight. "I'll be there shortly."

"Better make it yesterday, Kent. The mayor is really hot and he's coming down on Sam like gangbusters."

"Did you call Roger?"

"No way, man. I'm leaving that chore to you. The last time I got him up he blistered my ears every time he saw me for a week."

Jon laughed shortly, easily imagining Roger's ire. "Okay, I'll beard the lion in his den for you."

"I owe you one, buddy."

After breaking the connection, Jon swiftly dialed Roger's number. As predicted, his partner would have put a cornered wolverine to shame over having his sleep disturbed. After he uttered a round of blue-tinted curses, Roger agreed to meet Jon at the fire site. Jon replaced the receiver, rose and stretched before heading for the bathroom and a quick shower. If it hadn't been for the personal skirmishing going on between Sam and the mayor there would really be no need to rush. The damage had already been done and the forensic team from the fire department would have to go through the building first anyway. Frowning, Jon moved down the semidark hall to the kitchen. He needed coffee before he moved another inch.

His apartment was military neat with lots of wood furniture and rich colors. The one rather strange note in his home was the second bedroom, which was lined with bookshelves filled to overflowing. It was a miniature library complete with comfortable reading chair and light and one small table beside the chair on which reposed a carved pipe and humidor. The only other piece in the room was a table on which was spread a half-finished jigsaw puzzle. His two vices, a pipe with a book or a puzzle. Jon didn't own a television set, since he had no time to watch and even less inclination to try to make time. Mental exercise was his favorite sport. He still dated occasionally, needing the company of a woman but always keeping in mind his resolution of noninvolvement.

He poured himself a cup of coffee and looked around his home, suddenly struck by the loneliness of getting up in the middle of the night with no one to care he was tired, frustrated or just plain hungry for the sound of another human voice. Maybe he was becoming too solitary of late. The moment that thought was born, he had an image of green eyes and short, sassy dark brown hair framing a face too beautiful for ordinary words. Irritated at the swift vision, he shook his head. He was taking his curiosity about and admiration for Tracy Michaels too far. He'd be better off if he kept his mind on the job and his libido under wraps until the case was over and he was out of temptation's way.

Tracy stood in the shower as long as she dared, cursing herself for a fool for scrubbing the walkway on her hands and knees for three hours the night before.

She was stiff, sore in places she hadn't even known existed, and was in no mood to think up a hot topic for today's show. Finally, satisfied she was as loosened up as she was going to get, she turned off the water and stepped out. Drying, she decided to dress for comfort rather than executive style. A pair of white designer jeans and a scarlet blouse set off her slim figure. She pulled her dark brown hair back from her face with a pearl barrette. White low-heeled sandals felt as good as they looked. Downstairs, she popped bread in the toaster and poured herself a cup of coffee before settling down with the paper she had brought in earlier.

She frowned at the headlines. Nothing grabbed her interest. Irritated, she turned on the radio. It was almost time for the news at the top of the hour. A moment later her hand stilled in the process of spreading marmalade on her toast.

"The firebug lit up again this morning, this time taking out the county offices on Datura. There were no injuries, but the building was completely gutted. The police are asking anyone who may have any information to contact them on the hotline number. All information will be kept confidential and a reward is offered based on the importance of the tip."

Tracy frowned thoughtfully, wondering if Bo would call in again today. The professional side of her wanted the contact, but the personal side shied away from another meeting with Jon Kent. The man bothered her and no amount of pretending was making that fact any less real. Disgusted with her waffling, Tracy pushed away her half-eaten breakfast and got to her feet. Maybe the mental stimulation of work would do what cleaning her walk had not.

But even that was denied her. No sooner had she walked through the door of the radio station than she was met with at least three announcements that Jasper wanted to see her.

"I know, I know," she replied as Nikki added her voice to the group. "What's up? Do you know?"

"Not for sure. But at a guess I'd say a little call from a certain detective had something to do with it," Nikki said, studying Tracy closely. "You don't look too great. Have you been slaving over that house of yours again after work? You're going to kill yourself if you keep pushing so hard. It's time you got out and enjoyed yourself. I wish you'd let me introduce you to some nice man. Let one take you out to dinner, maybe to a play at the playhouse. Put a little fun in your life instead of work."

Tracy dropped her handbag in the bottom drawer of her desk and tried to stifle her irritation at the well-meant concern. "Not today, Nikki. I didn't get much sleep last night and I'm in a rotten mood."

"That ought to make Jasper's day," Nikki murmured as Tracy passed her friend's desk on the way to the station manager's office.

"I hope it will make someone's," Tracy returned, striving for a light note. A minute later she opened the door to Jasper's inner sanctum.

"It took you long enough to get here. You did hear the news on your way in, didn't you?" he muttered as he greeted her with a grumpy look.

Tracy took a seat before answering. "If you're referring to the hit by the firebug last night then yes, I heard."

"What do you plan to do about it?" he demanded.

Tracy's brows lifted at the question. "What should I do about it?" she returned.

"I got a call from Detective Kent. He's coming over here this morning. He wants you to do another show on the firebug. He's hoping that Bo character will call in again." Jasper leaned back in his chair, giving her a sharp look. "Normally, I wouldn't go along with anyone getting involved in our scheduling, but this is a special case. I want you to cooperate with the police."

In her youth, Tracy's temper had been of a very uncertain nature. Maturity and a few knocks taken because of her inability to restrain herself had taught her self-control. In a few words, Jasper had eaten away at the bonds that kept her disposition smooth and easy to work with.

"I hadn't planned on doing another show on this nut so soon."

She worked at being calm, neutral. Part of her realized the value her show might have, not just to the station, if they were instrumental in putting the firebug out of business, but to the public interest and her own credibility. The problem was more complex than that. She cared about her show and her professional integrity. Thus far she had never needed to compromise either, no matter how high-minded the reason.

The intercom buzzed, interrupting whatever Jasper might have said in rebuttal. "Detective Kent is here, boss," the receptionist announced.

"Send him in."

Tracy drew on every skill she knew to keep her expression smooth as she watched Jasper watching her. The office door opened behind her, but she didn't turn.

Jon felt the tension in the room the moment he walked in. It didn't take two guesses to know that Lynch had told Tracy of his plans for her show. "I'm sorry, I'm late. Got held up at the station." He walked to the chair beside Tracy's and sat down. He felt her glance in his direction but he kept his eyes on Jasper. "I assume that you have apprised Ms. Michaels of what we need."

"I have."

Both men looked at her. Tracy looked at only one. "I don't know if this is a good idea. I don't have a reputation for doing repeat shows. I gather the idea is to draw this firebug out, that is, assuming that Bo and the firebug are the same person. And that's a lot of assuming, given the facts so far." She ignored the flicker of admiration in Jon's black eyes for her deductions as she pressed on. "I would think a man as sharp as the firebug would be suspicious if I suddenly changed my mode of operation. He hasn't escaped all the people after him by being dense or stupid."

Jon inclined his head, having had the same doubts himself about the plan he, Roger and Sam had devised. "You're our only lead so far. We want this guy before he hurts someone. What if you turn us down and the next fire takes out an innocent person? How will you feel?" He was pushing but he was running out of time.

Tracy's temper slipped another notch. "That was a low blow."

"Perhaps, but I need your help."

"Antagonizing me won't get it."

"All of this is academic," Jasper cut in. "Tracy will do the show." His gray brows drew together in an irritated expression.

Jon shook his head before Jasper finished speaking. "We need cooperation, not force."

Tracy pulled up short, surprised at Jon's defense. All three of them knew Jasper had the power to command her agreement. Feeling curious when she would rather have stayed irritated, Tracy studied Jon. He looked back at her, making no attempt this time to influence her. "You really think it will work?" she asked slowly.

"I don't know. Like I said, you're all we've got. I don't like the fact that these last two jobs came so close together. I don't like the fact that you're getting these calls at all. I don't like knowing that all of the three police forces and the three fire teams investigating these jobs have come up empty."

"All right. I'll do the show."

Jon inclined his head, disturbed at the lack of satisfaction he felt on receiving her agreement. He should have been pleased; instead he was wishing he didn't have to involve her. Still, there should be little danger in the work she would be doing, so why was he worried?

Tracy got to her feet, eager to get away. "I have a show to do," she murmured, seizing the excuse.

"Is it all right if I watch?" Jon asked, rising.

"I think it would be a good idea," Jasper said. "Tracy will take care of you." He waved them out.

Left with no choice in the matter, Tracy kept pace with Jon as they walked back to the programmers' room. Neither spoke until they reached Tracy's desk.

The room was deserted for the moment. Jon laid his hand on her arm, surprised to feel the tension in her muscles. "I'm sorry I had to back you into a corner."

Tracy looked at his fingers next to the scarlet of her sleeve. His voice could be bottled and sold as a tranquilizer, it was so soothing, so calm. She envied him that ability. "Don't be. You were right. I wasn't." She gazed into his eyes, then wished she hadn't.

The look he gave her spoke of things beyond the case that temporarily bound them. A man's yearning stared out of those eyes, drawing her closer despite her best attempts to remain unmoved.

"Don't," she whispered, too shocked to pretend she didn't know he wanted her.

For one moment she thought he would ignore her plea, then he blinked and his lashes drifted down. He drew his hand slowly from her skin, making the gesture a caress rather than a simple movement. Tracy shivered, cold then hot in a room that was too comfortable in temperature for either sensation.

"Tell me about your show. How it works."

Tracy glanced past him, trying to collect herself to respond. The sight of Nikki entering the room had all the earmarks of a life preserver tossed to a drowning woman. "I don't have the time now, but Nikki would be glad to take you under her wing."

Nikki walked over, her face lighting with a puzzled smile. "What have you promised me for, my friend?"

"Jon needs a guide to show him around."

Jon watched the two women, seeing the difference in the pair. Nikki had an open expression, a kind of I-like-the-world look in her eyes that Tracy lacked. If life had ever dealt her a blow it wasn't visible. She

linked her arm with his and grinned at him as though
playing nursemaid was her favorite occupation.

"Come on, big guy. Let me teach you the ropes."

Jon found himself laughing when he had only
meant to be mildly amused. If he had had a sister he
would have liked one like Nikki. "Lead on. I'm all
yours." He glanced at Tracy, catching the flicker of
displeasure in her eyes before she veiled them. His
humor dimmed as he read the jealousy that shouldn't
have been there. But his own reaction stunned him
more than hers.

He was glad she was jealous. Damn! A man who
was capable of ignoring a woman wouldn't care that
she was jealous that he was smiling at someone else.
He swore again. This time the culprit was Roger and
his cold. If his partner had not gone home sick shortly
after arriving at their early-morning rendezvous at the
arson site, he could have avoided being in Tracy's
company. Instead, he had no choice.

He sat at the table, listening to the radio. Her voice
attracted him with its familiar slip of syllables. Home.
She reminded him of home and a time when he didn't
face the day driven by his nightmare. Firebug. He
smiled a little at the name. The media liked sensation-
alism. He touched the phone. He wanted to talk to her
again, wanted her to understand. She had been kind
to him the other times. He needed to talk to someone.
The end of it all was so close. He didn't know what he
would do when his mission was done. He needed
someone to care but there was no one any longer. Only
him. And only Tracy, the lady with the voice from

home and the kindness in her heart for everyone who called her. He reached for the phone. Why not? He could afford one more risk.

Chapter 3

Tracy took her place at the mike, trying not to notice how comfortable Nikki and Jon looked sitting side by side in the control room. At the moment neither was paying her any attention, as Nikki showed Jon how the computer and phone lines connected the host with the audience. Tracy put on her headset, irritated that she had chosen flight, albeit a subtle retreat, from Jon's influence. Nikki might have been fooled but Jon had not been. His eyes had held a hint of amusement and speculation that had made her regret the impulse of handing him over to Nikki. Tracy glanced at the director as her theme music came on. She began her intro, forcibly reminding herself that she would be better served to concentrate on her job and not on Jon Kent.

"She's very good," Jon murmured, watching Tracy handle the callers without a break. Listening to her on the radio was far different from seeing the professional at work. Tracy's ability to think on her feet was even more impressive when one saw her in person.

"She's dynamite," Nikki agreed as soon as she finished answering another line. "Of course, this firebug thing is a hot item right now. That helps. But I *have* seen her take a dull issue and turn it into something that demanded audience participation."

Jon glanced at her. "That's a nice compliment coming from someone who hosts the same type of show."

"It's the truth, and besides, Tracy and I are friends. I'm a very competitive person and I'll admit that when Tracy came out of Virginia to kind of take the West Palm Beach market by storm, I had a touch of the green-eyed virus. But I got over it. Tracy isn't the kind of person to step on people. She's a pro down to her toes and she doesn't mind sharing credit. I like her— in fact I don't think there's anyone here who doesn't." The phone rang again, interrupting them.

Jon digested the information as he turned his attention to Tracy. Every mood was reflected on her face when she was in front of the mike. She was by turns humorous, incisive and sympathetic. Yet when she had sat beside him in Jasper's office only the faint change of expression in her eyes had given him a clue to her thoughts. He wondered at the difference. Was it possible that she was as wary of him as he was of her? And if so, why?

"Has she got anyone special in her life?" Jon asked before he thought, a rare occurrence for him.

Nikki shot him a look that saw through the casual way he had put the question. "No, and not likely to right now, either."

Jon glanced at her, his interest redirected by her tone. "Why?"

"Why do you want to know?"

The blunt question took him by surprise. He shouldn't have started the conversation but now that he had, for better or worse, he'd stick it out. "She interests me," he admitted, opting for the least telling of his responses.

Nikki laughed softly. "Is that what you call it?"

He laughed with her. "In mixed company."

Out of the corner of her eye Tracy caught the humor that Jon and Nikki shared, feeling irritated with herself that she noticed and that she even cared. She almost missed the name of her next caller, which irritated her even more. Having Jon sitting in the control booth was not beneficial to her show or her temperament. Time had never passed so slowly on a subject that should have held her interest. When the break in the middle of the two-hour show finally arrived, she was more than ready to pull off the headset and get out of her chair. What she wasn't ready for was Jon entering the room, carrying a cup of hot tea.

"Nikki said you might be able to use this," he said, passing her the cup before taking the chair across from her. He glanced around the small enclosure, noting the electronic equipment. On the right was another room similar to the one he had just left. "This is amazing. It's too bad we haven't made as good a use of our space at the police station."

Tracy was more than glad to accept the neutral topic. "Necessity from what I hear. This used to be a single family residence. Not much was done to it when the radio station took the place over—no money, I guess. A few partitions were put up here and there. Personally, this place reminds me of a rabbit warren."

Jon laughed softly, liking her description. "Now that you mention it, it does." He studied her, tipping his head to one side. "You make a cute bun—"

"Don't say it," she warned, surprised at her need to laugh with him. "Even if I did leave myself open for it." The director's signal caught her eye. She sighed regretfully, though she wasn't sure why, that their time was over. "Gotta get back to work."

Jon took her empty cup, his fingers brushing hers. When she didn't draw away immediately, neither did he. "We both do." Even he could hear the regret in his voice.

Tracy pulled her hand from beneath his, trying to keep her expression calm when her heart had suddenly developed a disconcerting rhythm. She was not ready for this! "You'd better go," she murmured, mentally cursing the suddenly husky note in her voice.

Jon rose, damning the need to touch more than her hand. He was no male on the make. This kind of reaction was not his style. He liked slow and easy relationships where both people knew the rules. "Let's hope we have better luck this next hour." He needed a reminder as to why he was there with her.

Tracy inclined her head. "I've got my fingers crossed," she agreed, but not for the reason he might think. She didn't watch him leave, rather she busied

herself with unnecessary electronic adjustments until
it was time for her to open the lines again. The second
hour was even busier than the first. She didn't have a
moment to look Jon's way or to consider her reactions to the man.

Finally it was time for the last call of the day.
"Hello, Bob, you're on the air."

"My name's not Bob, it's Bo. Do you remember
me, Tracy?"

Tracy's eyes sought Jon's. He gave her an encouraging nod to continue. Oddly, she was nervous when
she hadn't expected to be. "What have you got for me,
Bo?" she asked carefully.

"I saw the fire last night."

Her brows rose, but her eyes stayed fixed on Jon.
She saw him stiffen and say something to Nikki.
"How?" Tracy prompted.

"I was there. Whole thing went up like a torch. That
guy is really good."

"Which guy?"

He sighed, clearly irritated at the question. "You
know who I'm talking about. The firebug. He has the
police running in circles."

"You sound like you admire him."

"I do. He's smart and he doesn't hurt people."

"Don't you think burning down a person's business hurts?"

"Yeah, in the pocketbook for a time. Then insurance steps in and nothing is different." No one could
mistake his disgust at the system.

"What would you like to be different?" she probed,
playing a hunch. She debated asking the man outright if he were the firebug and decided against it.

"I'd like justice."

Startled, she hesitated. "For whom?"

"The little guys that make these big guys big."

Without another word he hung up. Tracy smoothed the abrupt ending, needing only to stretch her closing remarks for a few seconds before her theme music took over. Jon was in the room before she could remove her headset.

"Are you all right?" he demanded.

"Why wouldn't I be?" She evaded the hand he extended. There were too many people around and, whether she admitted it or not, she was shaken by the call.

Jon frowned and tucked his hand in his pocket. "It looks as if he's hooked." He stepped back so that she could pass him.

"You should be glad."

"So should you. It won't hurt your credibility any to help us catch this guy," he retorted, stung at her inference.

Ignoring the taunt, Tracy stopped in the hall to study him. "Now what? I can't keep doing shows on the firebug forever."

"I know. We'll think of something else."

"*You'll* think of something," she corrected, heading for her desk. "I just obey orders."

Jon followed, not liking the irritation that still rode her at the way Jasper had chosen to force her cooperation, cooperation he was positive they would have had anyway, if she had been given a choice. "You don't follow orders with me. You know this business. I don't."

She flopped in her chair, wondering what he was up to. She didn't trust his innocent look. "Meaning?"

"I think it would help if we got together and decided on a course of action, and I don't think the place to do it is here." He glanced significantly around the crowded room where privacy was nonexistent.

"Where would this meeting take place?" she asked suspiciously.

"Over dinner might be nice," he said, hoping she would relax. If he had half a brain he wouldn't have made the suggestion, but now that the words were said he didn't regret them.

"That's an interesting approach to asking me out," she observed.

"I thought so." He took a seat. "Going to take me up on it? I promise you I know some great restaurants."

Unable to help herself, she laughed. "I told Nikki your partner wasn't the more dangerous of the two of you. Now I know I'm right."

Jon wasn't about to let her know how much her words pleased him. "Is that a yes or a no?"

Tracy's amusement dimmed, replaced with an intensity her co-workers would have recognized. "If you really mean the invitation the way it was given, with maybe a little polite flirting thrown in, then all right. Otherwise no."

Jon digested the warning. His admiration of her character rose even higher. This was a woman for truths, not game playing. "I like honesty. I'm glad you do, too. I'm attracted to you and I don't trust it any more than you seem to. I can't give you any better answer but either way we still have to deal with the firebug. For the moment that means we have to deal with each other.''

''Good point.'' She smiled slightly, liking his ability to give her the honesty she needed. ''What time would you like me to be ready?''

''Seven?''

''Know my address?''

He nodded without explaining that it was in the research he had done on her.

''Dressy or casual?''

''Dressy. I don't go out much. When I do, I like to know it.''

She smiled, sharing his feelings. Excitement for the evening ahead flickered to life, deepening her smile. For a moment she forgot what had brought them together and saw only a man who could stir her emotions. The look in Jon's eyes touched the basic part of her nature. She felt flattered, curious and very feminine. Jon's strength of will, of person, of behavior was so honestly male that she had never felt more female.

''You look shell-shocked,'' Nikki remarked as soon as the waiter departed with their luncheon order. She sipped her glass of white wine, idly listening to the buzz of the noontime crowd in the small restaurant that was so popular with the downtown workers.

''I hope you're the only one who's noticed.'' Tracy leaned back in her chair, trying to relax. She was wired from both the firebug investigation and the man she hardly knew but couldn't forget. The reaction was not a good combination in her job, where one needed every ounce of energy just to stay on schedule.

"I can almost guarantee that. With the things that have been going on at the station today, I don't think anyone would notice if a bomb dropped in the lobby. Bo sure has generated a lot of listener interest. The switchboard is about to blow a fuse." Nikki lifted her glass to her lips. "I thought you looked kind of funny when you handed Jon over to me this morning. What's wrong?"

Tracy glanced at Nikki. Her hopes that her friend had not picked up on her mood were wasted. "You're going to think I'm nuts," she murmured.

"It happens to all of us at one time or another." Nikki shrugged, momentarily looking less than her usually sunny self. "Is it that tall, dark drink of male water that sent me and the secretaries into a state of sexual shock? Or is it that sleepy-eyed bear who sat at my elbow all morning and treated me like his favorite aunt? If it were me it would be the first, but I bet it's Jon Kent for you."

Tracy tipped her head, curious despite herself. "Why?"

"Roger Landis might look dangerous but I have a feeling what you see is what you get. He'd be a good lover but he strikes me as a flirt." Both women heard the bitter note in Nikki's voice.

"Sounds like you've been there."

"In spades. Won't go again if I can help it. I don't mind telling you Detective Landis made more of an impression than I liked, but I'll get over it." She propped her elbow on the table and fixed Tracy with a sharp look. "But my love life isn't the issue. Yours is. What gives with Kent?"

Tracy shrugged, wishing she had kept her own counsel. "I don't know. He bothers me."

Nikki laughed, but not unkindly. "Only you could drawl those three words out in such a way as to give me ideas of hot nights and satin bed sheets."

"Your sense of humor leaves a lot to be desired," Tracy retorted, torn between laughter and annoyance.

"So I've been told."

"So what do I do?"

"If you're asking me a question like that, you are in a bad way." She frowned as she studied Tracy. "What's so wrong with finding the man interesting? You're free and so is he as far as I know."

"I don't want to get involved right now." She hesitated, then decided to confide her past. Nikki listened without interrupting, her expression in turns sympathetic and enraged for Tracy's sake.

"Some days it doesn't pay to get out of bed," she said sympathetically when Tracy finished. "I'll grant you this Lee creep was a bad break, but I don't see anything in Jon to make you draw any parallels."

"I'm not drawing parallels as much as trying to put the pieces together again. Lee shook my confidence. I don't trust my judgment anymore."

"Well, you can't hide forever," Nikki pointed out. "So what's the alternative? Let a tasty man slip away because you've suddenly discovered the dating game doesn't come with guarantees?"

"I want to get my house in order, get my career set, then look around."

"Sounds pretty cold-blooded to me."

Hearing the words out loud, Tracy was inclined to agree. "I hadn't thought of it that way," she defended herself automatically.

"I didn't either when something similar happened to me. I hibernated for about a year, and watched life from the outside, until one day I realized I wasn't getting any younger or any smarter about men, only more lonely. It made me angry. I realized then that although I had broken up with my creep I might as well have stayed with him, because I was being faithful without the advantage of a physical relationship," she said bluntly.

Tracy grimaced at the picture but couldn't deny the truth.

"So my best advice would be to go for it. Forget the past and concentrate on the present."

"How's the case going?" Sam leaned back in his chair and chewed on his unlit cigarette. "I listened to the show this morning. I'll give the woman credit, she handled herself well."

Ignoring the provocative statement, Jon took out his notebook, more out of habit than need. "The thing is what do we do for an encore? Tracy can't keep doing shows on the firebug. Even if the public will stand for it, our guy will get suspicious."

Sam tossed a paper across the desk to Jon. "Here's the tap-and-trace order duly signed by the judge. We'll tap her home phone and the office phone. But not the call-in lines because the general public's right to privacy would be violated. With this guy going to the trouble of disguising his voice and, from what you tell me, also giving sound-alike names to the person screening the calls we can't even isolate him enough to get him on a single line."

Jon swore.

"My feelings exactly. The judge won't budge. I tried everything."

"Tracy's not in the phone book, though her number's listed with the operator. She arrived in town too late for this year's edition. What makes you think this kook will bother her at home?" Jon had his own hunches but he wanted to hear Sam's.

The older man frowned deeply. "I don't like the way the guy sounds. It isn't that he uses Tracy's first name, most of her audience does that. It's the way he talks to her. There's something about his tone that bothers me."

"I agree. I also think there's something in that justice comment Bo made today. So far we haven't gotten much of a handle on this guy, because everyone has been treating it as a regular arson thing. Supposing it isn't? Supposing he isn't just a kook who gets his kicks watching things burn. Let's say for a minute the man feels he has a score to settle."

"Over three cities and more than a dozen businesses, none of which are related to each other?" Sam muttered skeptically.

"Think about it. The torch breezes into a city and out again, apparently without motive. Why would he quit setting fires in one place if watching something burn was his only motive? He has to know that he's running rings around the investigative teams. Why change cities? There has to be a reason. I want to talk to our psychologist, run my theory by him and see what he comes up with."

"You're taking a mighty big deductive jump."

Jon's lips twisted in a grim smile. "That's what I get paid to do, to think like a criminal and solve the puzzle of a warped mind." Jon rose, while tucking his notebook in his pocket. "One other thing—I don't think it's a good idea to count on Tracy in this mess. If this guy is out for revenge of some kind, he isn't going to be happy with whoever stops him. She's too easy a target."

Sam gave him a sharp look from beneath bushy brows. "We may not have any choice if this thing continues to go down the way it has so far. She's our only lead. Besides, with you around, she should be safe enough, and if it gets hot we'll assign a team to cover her. You know the drill. You've done it before."

"Not since my days undercover," Jon returned sharply, angered at the advice when he should have been able to take it in stride. He knew Sam, understood his blunt ways and his tough approach. Sam was honest to his bones, but he let nothing stop him from catching his man.

"You were good. You haven't forgotten the ropes," Sam replied just as quickly.

"I haven't forgotten. I just choose not to remember." Jon shifted, feeling a useless rage build for the past he couldn't change. He had never gotten over the occasional need to involve civilians in the fight to clean up the streets. He had seen too much not to know the risks. He had even paid the costs too many times to be forgotten.

"Because of Amanda?"

"Drop it, Sam. Even our friendship has limits."

Sam ignored the warning. "You can't keep feeling guilty forever. Her death was an accident. You know that. Every precaution had been taken."

"I lost more than Amanda." Jon's eyes darkened with painful memories, memories only a few people had the courage to call up.

"The child."

"*My* child."

"Other men have lost those they cared about."

Jon glanced at the squad room with eyes that were bleak. "We both know how they deal with the pain. I chose my way so let it be. I work and I don't drink, or use women like tissues or find peace in medically prescribed tranquilizers. And I also didn't work myself so deep into the ground that I ended up burned out at thirty."

"You did cut yourself off. When is the last time you really cared about someone?"

Jon smiled grimly. "You might ask yourself the same question," he said before walking out the door and shutting it quietly behind him. He needed an outlet for the emotions he usually kept under tight wraps. Sam had lanced wounds that still hadn't healed. His stride lengthened, eating up the yards from the station to the parking lot. His driving verged on reckless as he headed for the psychologist who served in an advisory capacity for their investigations. The receptionist smiled at him when he entered. He barely noticed.

"You look like you want to hit someone," William Lindquist, better known as Doc, commented as soon as Jon sat down.

"Namely Sam."

Doc chuckled and leaned back in his chair. "That explains it. If that man has a subtle bone in his body I haven't found it."

"Neither have I and I've known him longer than you."

"So what is it this time?"

"The firebug."

Doc's brows rose, his eyes alive with interest. "Tell me."

Jon proceeded to give him an account of every fact to date then asked, "What's the possible connection with Tracy?"

"Maybe she's got a familiar voice. Frequently, lonely people become attached to public figures, seeing them as friends in a life empty of real connections. Maybe he's physically drawn to her. She sounds sexy over the air. That could be a turn-on, assuming of course that her caller and the firebug are the same man."

"What's the danger to her if she gets in any deeper?"

"Your guess is as good as mine at this point. I agree with you in that I don't think this is a regular torch situation. People who step out of patterns are erratic, unpredictable. She could be in danger, depending on the kind of fixation your man has. Anyone who gets close to her could be in an equal amount of trouble. You haven't found a motive yet?"

"No. We're starting to check with other states now. Getting anything substantial from them is a long shot but it's not impossible."

Doc tapped his pencil on the desk top, thinking. "Sam may be right in one thing. You should stick close to Tracy until you have a better picture. It wouldn't be too hard for her caller to follow her home from work, find where she lives and bother her, if not hurt her, if he gets spooked.''

Jon left the office with Doc's words ringing in his ears. Fate seemed to be conspiring to throw him in the same arena with Tracy. He had accepted difficult assignments in his life but this one was turning into a real winner. He was damned if he did and consigned to hell if he didn't.

"Wonderful choice, Kent," he muttered as he got in the car to head home to get ready for his dinner date.

The man stood in the shadows watching the building across the street. How many times had he waited in the shadows, thinking and planning his moves? His work was almost done. He'd traveled so many miles since he left home. So many strange beds, empty nights with only his dream to keep him going. That woman, Tracy, had touched a nerve in him with her show this morning. Those people who had called in hadn't cared why he'd set the fires. They'd only worried about what he'd done. Fools. Like the police. They looked for him but couldn't see him, even as he stood here in broad daylight, a hundred yards from his next target.

Tracy Michaels. She was from his home state. Did she miss it as he did? Virginia was so green, soft without the glare and the glitz of Florida. People were kinder there, more family oriented. He wanted to go home. But there was no home to go back to, no one to remember he had left or to know why. He was alone now. The need to finish was growing by the day. He wanted the mission over. He wanted peace.

Pushing away from the building that sheltered him from sight, he walked to his car. He had one more stop to make. He wanted to see Tracy Michaels in person. Her picture, the one in the newspaper, was no longer enough. He wanted to see her home, to think of her there. He needed to remember his own home, the price he had paid to start on his mission. But to find her home, he had to follow her from work. Another risk, this time for himself. He smiled grimly. The police wouldn't think he would be foolish enough to expose himself this way. That was his protection. As long as he did the unexpected he was safe.

Chapter 4

Tracy stared at her closet, debating what to wear. The green Hawaiian print dress matched with a pair of white sandals would be good. Of course, the scarlet-and-gold-dragon cotton was just as nice, but maybe that side slit halfway up her thigh was too sexy. At first her hand settled on the green, but it was the red that ultimately embraced her body, stroking over the flare of her hips as the gold dragon wrapped sinuously around her from breast to thigh. Her hair was loose, brushing the high neckline that was deceptively restrained until the moment she turned around to display the bare back from her neck to the base of her spine. Small cap sleeves were edged in gold as was the slit on the left side. Her lightly tanned legs had never looked longer or more shapely. Gold and garnet studs in her ears, a touch of red to her lips and gold and brown to her eyes and she looked definitely sexy and very elegant. The doorbell rang before she could lose her nerve and decide to change.

When Tracy opened the door, she caught her breath in surprise at the impact of seeing Jon again. In his casual working garb he had been masculine, dominant without being dominating. But tonight he was a danger to any woman with blood in her veins. He stood on her porch, watching her without saying a word. He didn't need to. Those eyes said everything any woman would have liked to hear and more.

Jon glanced over her, enjoying the rise of color in her cheeks, the way her lips parted although she said nothing. He could see the surprise in her eyes and wondered vaguely at the cause. Was she feeling the same slam of need as he? He realized in amazement that he hoped so. He didn't want this to be a one-sided attraction. He wanted her to want to know him as much as he wanted her to desire him. With the others in his life—not that there had been that many—it hadn't mattered.

Knowing he had been staring too long, he searched for a light comment, something to put a smile on her lips and ease the tension in her body. "You have style, Tracy Michaels. And great legs." His gaze returned to her face and he smiled. "But there's something wrong."

Tracy shook her head slightly, striving to clear it of Jon's influence. "There is? What?" Damn, the green dress would have been a better choice. He made her feel like the main course in a gourmet banquet, the prized gem in a collection of priceless jewels. She wanted to preen, to touch him and to have him touch her. She was certifiably crazy, she told herself as she took a step back.

Jon followed her step with one of his own. "Your mama didn't teach you any manners. You usually ask a guest in, not keep him standing on your front porch without so much as a greeting. Especially—" he pulled the hand he had hidden behind his back into view "—when said guest has brought you a present." He had thought about flowers although they were almost an outdated practice these days but the idea hadn't fit. He wanted something different. A gift shop, run by a friend, had been the answer.

Tracy looked from his face to the tiny figure in his hand. It was a sleek rendition of a woman standing in front of a microphone. The figure was in pewter mounted on a piece of amethyst geode. The purple crystals were beautiful by themselves but combined with the delicate metalwork the whole was a piece of art. "It's lovely," she murmured, too overcome by surprise to take the gift.

Jon smiled at her reaction, pleased that he had caught her off guard. Stepping close, he reached for her hand and tucked the figure into it. "She reminded me of you," he said huskily, wishing he dared kiss her.

Tracy looked up into his eyes, reading his wish and silently echoing it. "I have just the place for it," she whispered, a catch in her voice. She couldn't remember the last time anyone had brought her something without a reason. Part of her was melting inside because Jon, a near-stranger, had been the one to touch her so easily. "I've been remodeling the house," she hurried to explain, needing to get out of deep water before she betrayed herself. "I'll put it over the mantel of the small fireplace in my bedroom." The moment the words left her mouth, Tracy cursed her wayward tongue.

Jon's smile widened and he raised his hand to touch her cheek. "Tell me about your house," he suggested, easily recognizing her discomfort and finding he wanted to put her at ease. They had all the time they wanted to get to know each other.

Tracy looked into his eyes, off balance at the change of subject. "Now?" she asked.

"I think so unless you'd like me to ask to see where you're going to put my little present," he returned gruffly.

Tracy encircled his wrist with her free hand, stopping the fingers that were caressing her cheek. Her skin felt warm everywhere he touched. "I'm doing the work myself," she said absently, watching the way his eyes followed her words.

"Is that out of necessity or because you like doing the work?"

"A bit of both."

"I don't think I would have attempted this place on my own. I'm not the world's most coordinated man with tools."

Tracy smiled at the rueful tone, discovering she liked being close to Jon, listening to his voice, feeling the desire ripple gently through her without driving her into a situation that she wasn't ready for. "I find that hard to believe."

He succumbed to the temptation to drop a light kiss on her lips, then he stepped away before she could object. "You should have been around when I tried to fix a leak in the kitchen faucet the day the apartment maintenance man was off. I had to pay to have the ceiling replaced in the apartment below mine. I turned the wrong water control thing off."

Tracy laughed, picturing the scene. "I don't know anyone else who would admit that," she said before she thought.

Chuckling, Jon shrugged. "If you can't do something, so what. There's enough around I *can* do that I don't worry about making a fool of myself by trying to be an expert in all areas. I always thought perfection was boring and a perfectionist damn hard to live with."

The last of Tracy's tension over the coming evening took a vacation to Siberia. Men, in her limited experience, wanted to appear perfect in all situations. Yet this one wasn't above admitting a human frailty without apologizing for it.

It would have been so easy to reach out and touch her again. Jon balled his fists in his pockets and resisted the urge. He had come out of curiosity and attraction. He was finding a need to know the woman and the wanting that came with that knowledge. If he had been the type of man to turn from a challenge he would have now. Tracy, with her clear green eyes and her smile like a rainbow after a storm, was shaking up his life.

"I don't suppose you'd like a helper in your remodeling? I may not be great but I work cheap."

Tracy saw beyond Jon's words. He was as wary about their attraction as she was, although she didn't know why. "Are you sure?"

"No, but I won't retract the offer," he replied honestly.

Tracy found humor in the distracted response. His feelings were so close to her own. Laughing softly, she placed her statue on the coffee table for the evening and picked up her bag. "You have a way of getting to my ego. Don't you know anything about white lies?"

"No," he admitted. "I avoid them at all costs. Probably has something to do with my work. I spend too much time in the criminal maze of half-truths and complete fabrications. I don't want it in my real life."

Startled, Tracy glanced at him in surprise. "You sound as if you don't like what you do."

"I do like the challenge of solving the crimes, but no, I can't say that I actually like what I do so much as I am committed to it."

She nodded, watching the light shift gently over his face. His eyes were deep, filled with hidden meanings. "I think I understand a little. I've seen your face when you're talking about this case. You forget the world while you twist and turn in the maze this firebug is weaving."

"That bothers a lot of people."

"Not me. I get the same kind of tunnel vision." She waved her hand at the room. "Take this place, for instance. Nikki says I'm well on my way to being obsessive."

He touched her then, not liking the faint flicker of hurt in her eyes. "Committed," he disagreed, tucking her hand in his. "I recognize the symptoms," he continued at her surprised look. "That's why I took up a hobby. You fix up this house and I put together puzzles."

"That sounds a bit like a busman's holiday to me," she pointed out, suddenly needing to put some emotional if not physical distance between them. His smile was kind but knowing.

"It is and it isn't." He drew her toward the door. "Ask me again next time and I may show you one of my puzzles."

"That implies we'll have a second date."

He waited while she said goodbye to her dog and locked the door. "I want one. I hope you do, too, but only for the right reasons." He reached out to touch her cheek, his fingers lingering on the soft curve. "We've been thrown into a situation that may distort our values and beliefs. I've been there but you haven't. Be careful."

Tracy stared into his eyes, seeing strength and power she had never known in anyone else. "Is that a warning?" In another time, with someone else, she might have objected strenuously to such plain speaking. With Jon, she respected his need and her own to lay facts on the line.

"Yes. It's for myself as well as you. I'm attracted to you—you're woman enough to know it—and I think you're attracted to me. I won't lie to you, ever, for any reason."

"And I won't lie to you." She wrapped her fingers around his wrist, feeling his pulse throb with life. "I wasn't looking for someone and I don't trust easily these days."

"Neither do I."

"It would be easier if you walked away."

"I don't think I can. Can you?"

"I wish I could," she answered slowly.

"Then we'll go forward." He lifted his hand from the warmth of her skin.

Tracy released her hold at the same time as he did. Cool night air replaced the heat of his flesh. Tension eased from her body, relaxing her muscles. She smiled, feeling free without understanding why.

Jon caught her smile and shared it. He knew it was too easy for him to like this woman. He needed a bit of space, so he chose a neutral topic of conversation. "Tracy, how did you come by that dog of yours? I've never seen such an odd-looking animal in my life."

Tracy's explanation of Handsome's short stint in a small Virginia town's dog pound took them into the car and on the interstate to West Palm Beach.

"Where are we going?" Tracy turned sideways in her seat so that she could watch Jon drive. He handled the car with controlled finesse. She appreciated the lack of showiness.

"To a very special place I know. I hope you like it." He glanced at her, admiring the way the streetlights illuminated the elegant lines and hollows of her face.

"I'll give it my best shot, especially if the food is good. I'm starved."

He laughed. "Going to put a dent in my bank balance, are you?"

Smiling, she settled back in her seat to enjoy the ride. For this moment their intense physical attraction was on hold. The silence was easy, the tension that had invaded her home with Jon's arrival blunted to a kind of companionship Tracy found relaxing.

"Tell me about your work and as much as you can about the firebug," she invited.

"My work is basically taking bits and pieces of information and arranging them in a coherent form. Tedious, irritating, challenging and frustrating would make good job descriptions—depending on the day. I've been at it for about twelve years. Roger and I got the firebug case because the fire marshal's office isn't having much luck with the thing. While they have the ability to make arrests, and they certainly have done a great job sifting through the debris to get information on the device and method of entry into the buildings hit so far, they don't have quite the manpower to work on this aspect of the case. That's where my department comes in."

"Are there any leads?"

"A couple. The guy's been bypassing the burglar and fire alarms, so he may have some electronics experience. In one case, there was a local alarm but that was ignored until it was too late. His methods vary but he always uses materials that are readily available in any store. He also has some knowledge of how best to make a building burn."

"What do you mean? I thought burning was burning."

"I wish." He sighed. "Most of our construction down here is concrete block. Set up the right way, a fire in this type of structure can become a giant chimney. Fire needs three things to burn well: a source of fuel, ignition and oxygen. Our torch understands this fact and uses it to the best advantage. So far every place he's hit has been gutted."

"Maybe he was a fireman at one point."

"We thought of that, but so far we haven't found anyone on our city, county or state rosters that we couldn't clear."

"Maybe he's from another state."

"We're checking that now." He smiled at her last suggestion. "I don't suppose you'd like a job? You're good at piecing together things."

"One or two good guesses don't give me any urge to take on your kind of work. I think I'd make a worse detective than you say you'd make a plumber." Tracy laughed a little at her curiosity and inability to leave the subject alone then sobered. "Why do you think he's doing this? Attention? Or is he someone who just enjoys watching fire destroy things?"

"Based on the little info we've been able to give him, the police department psychologist doesn't think our man fits the normal profile of a torch."

"Oh, so where does that leave you?"

"With you."

Startled, Tracy stared at him, watching the grin curve his lips. "You know, you're a very deceptive person," she murmured. That wiped the amusement from his face.

"How?"

"I could have sworn you didn't have much of a sense of humor when I met you. Your partner certainly doesn't."

"Roger tends to bite first. Plus he's fighting a cold and exhaustion at the moment. The last case we were on was a real witch," he explained, troubled by her assessment when he shouldn't have been. "Did you really think that?"

She nodded. "You brought that notebook out, poked your nose in the pages and scribbled away every time I opened my mouth. Your friend Roger looked as if he wanted to glare at Jasper or me most of the time. And when you did look up you looked bored."

"Bored? I was not." That was impossible. He distinctly remembered spending most of the interview trying not to notice how beautiful Tracy was, and how much deeper and sexier her voice sounded when it wasn't changed by the microphone.

"What were you then?"

Jon greeted their arrival at their destination with relief. If he answered that question, Tracy would find a job in Alaska before the night was over. "Saved by the bell," he muttered under his breath. Her soft chuckle told him she had heard.

"I'll let you off the hook this time," she teased as they got out of the car.

"I tell you what. I'll give you a rain check you can redeem later if you still want to know."

The darkness around them was soft and scented. The wanting was back, stronger and more dangerously beguiling than ever. Tracy fought the pull enough to steady her voice. "A rain check it is."

Jon touched her arm in his with a faint smile. "Ever heard of a progressive date?"

Tracy gazed at the popular night spot, then back at Jon's face. She started to call him on his obvious evasion but changed her mind. One good look at his expression told her all she needed to know. He was as much a prisoner of the strange chemistry between them as she. He was making an attempt to slow the process down and she wanted to help them both by going along with him.

"No. Is it a game?"

The lady was smart as well as beautiful. "Sort of. Every part of the evening has a different locale. I thought you might enjoy it."

"So we start here for drinks," she guessed.

"Then over to a little spot I know in Palm Beach. They have the best shrimp scampi in the county if you like seafood."

"I do."

"Then to another small restaurant that specializes in the best coffee you've ever tasted and the most fantastic desserts this side of heaven. After that we can work off the extra calories at a dance place in North Palm Beach that has a live big band sound."

"I think puzzles aren't the only things you like to do. You seem very good at planning."

"Do you mind? We can do something else if you'd rather."

"Not on your life. I never would have thought about picking the best of each thing then moving on. It's a wonderful idea."

Jon stopped in a small, secluded curve in the sidewalk that was surrounded by lush tropical foliage. With one arm he pulled her closer. Using his free hand, he stroked her cheek, then moved it down the side of her neck to rest at the base of her throat. "I'm going to kiss you. Are you going to let me?"

Tracy caught her breath at the question. Would she have done nothing to stop him had he simply taken her lips? "That's not fair."

"What's not?" He moved closer, drawn by her scent, the softness in her eyes.

"You aren't supposed to ask." She leaned nearer, unable to resist the temptation to touch him.

"Why not? I don't want to sneak up on your blind side and I'm not much good at maneuvering women into clinches. Never wanted to learn. Submissiveness never appealed to me." He wrapped his hand lightly around her neck, his fingers sliding under the collar to stroke her skin. It was warm, satiny smooth and addictive.

Tracy stared into his eyes, losing a piece of herself in their black depths. Her lips parted, her body softening as warmth spread from his hand to her limbs.

"Your eyes are shining, do you know that?" he whispered, bending his head to brush her lips. "You taste sweet. And covering skin like yours is against the laws of nature." His fingers dipped lower, barely brushing the top of the scrap of lace that cupped her breast.

Tracy inhaled sharply at the touch, aching in places she hadn't felt in a long time. She wanted more. His tongue probed gently at her mouth, touching then retreating, inviting her to play. She kissed him back, arching against him, ever conscious of his hand. It never moved, just stayed tantalizingly poised as her nipples hardened in rebellion at being denied their due.

Jon lifted his head, pleased at the flush on her cheeks and the way she reached for him. He was hurting but the pain was sweet, a promise of delights to come.

"Are you ready to go in?"

"You're crazy. Now?" Her words emerged in an unsteady whisper.

"You would rather stay here?"

"I see that smile and it looks too satisfied for safety," she murmured, leaning back so that his hand slipped from her dress with agonizing slowness.

"Not satisfied, sweetheart. Not by a long shot." He eased away without breaking contact with her. "You look very kissed."

"You mean I look like I came through a bush backward." Tracy wasn't sure what had happened, but with the way Jon was handling the situation she found she wasn't embarrassed by her lack of control. His eyes held a twinkle of amusement but there was no malice in them and she was certain his humor was directed as much at himself as her.

"No protests that I took advantage of you?"

"You made sure of that when you asked me if I minded a kiss," she replied, finding it easier by the second to damp down the desire that had built during the moments in his arms. "By the way, that was a sneaky trick."

"I am never sneaky," Jon protested, enjoying her recovery and her strength. She was all woman, and he was fast coming to the conclusion he had to have her soon. He had started with liking her wit and intelligence on her show, progressed to finding her beautiful. Now her taste was on his lips and the memory of the feel of her body pressed against his was imprinted in his mind.

Desire. A friend or an enemy. Tonight a willing ally.

"You may not think you are, but I've got news, you are."

"And you're sexy as sin," he retaliated as they entered the nightclub.

Rich blues, dark greens and gold combined with real wood paneling to create a quiet oasis for the couples at small tables around the room. There was a circular bar in the center, where half the stools were taken. Jon cupped Tracy's elbow, guiding her to a quiet corner screened by an extravagant assortment of plants. The waitress was there before they even sat down. She moved a reserved sign from the middle of the table.

Tracy waited until their order was taken before saying, "I didn't realize tables could be reserved in a place like this."

"They can't. This just happens to be my favorite spot in the room."

"So they save it for you?" Her brows rose, daring him to try to scrape through with such a lame excuse.

"Not exactly. A friend of mine owns the place."

"Neat move."

"I thought so. I'm working on impressing you."

"Is that what it's called?" Tracy would have continued, but she was interrupted.

"Jon, I thought there had to be a special reason for you dropping by. Now I see what it is."

Tracy turned her head to watch the approach of a man tall enough to have played pro basketball. A thatch of unruly blond hair topped a lanky frame that looked surprisingly elegant in a dark brown sport jacket, cream shirt and tie and butterscotch-colored slacks.

"I was hoping you'd be off somewhere amusing yourself this evening," Jon said, moving his chair closer to Tracy's to give the newcomer room to join them.

"Out of luck, buddy." He extended his hand to Tracy, blue eyes bright with enthusiasm and mischief. "I'm Davy. Full name, David Hawthorne Roman Knight. And you are..." He cocked his head, waiting.

"Tracy Michaels." She placed her hand in his, laughing when he carried it to his lips with the flourish of nobility.

"Glad to meet you, Tracy. Where did you meet this misbegotten son of Satan?"

"Jon?" Her brows rose at the description.

"She must be new. She doesn't know you very well yet," Davy said to Jon.

"And she won't if you keep on, you great tower. Would you shut up before I forget I'm a gentleman."

"Now, you know you don't mean that, little man."

Tracy choked on a laugh. "Little man?" she gasped out when she could speak.

"Well, he is to me," Davy pointed out. "I'm six-eleven and he's six-two. I beat him by nine inches."

"Outweigh me, too."

"We won't discuss that. I'm on a diet." He paused to smile at the waitress who brought their drinks.

"You should be locked up, boss," the woman said before departing with a grin.

"*You* own this place?" Tracy asked.

"For my sins. Didn't Jon tell you?"

"Not exactly." Tracy shot Jon a look.

Jon spread his hands, denying culpability. "I haven't had time with you two hogging the show."

"We could leave him. I think you'd like me better anyway. I don't run around with a puzzle tucked under my arm and my nose buried in a book."

It was an old argument. "I'm not that bad," Jon protested.

Davy ignored him. "So tell me, pretty lady, what do you do?"

Jon laughed. "Did you slip this time, my friend? Don't you recognize her name?"

Davy frowned, glancing first at Jon then back at Tracy. "That Tracy Michaels?"

"How many do you think there are running around the city?" Jon asked.

Davy ignored the interruption. "I listen to your show."

"When you're awake."

"You know, listening to you two is like watching a tennis match. Do either of you hear the other?" Tracy demanded, trying not to laugh aloud at the way each scored in the verbal battle.

"Of course."

"My best friend."

The two answers held equal measures of indignation.

"This guy is the one who went partners with me in the Hawk's Nest. I wouldn't have this place at all if it weren't for Jon."

"You talk too much. Why is it I always end up with people in my life who would sell their soul to the devil?"

"Just lucky."

Tracy leaned back, seeing that coherent conversation with this pair was out of the question. When she had agreed to this date she'd had some preconceived ideas about Jon. Now she'd gotten a glimpse of a man she'd never expected. He baffled her as he seemed to slip into different personas at will. While he usually looked as if a bomb under his chair wouldn't disturb him, he planned an evening that was anything but staid and conventional. He had kissed her on the walk in full view of anyone who cared to look, as though they had been alone in a room with all the time in the world to get to know each other. He had demanded she know what she wanted before he touched her. He could have taken and given more, and yet he had not.

And his best friend was an unabashed extrovert who ran an elegant establishment but didn't look as if he had done a day's work in his life. Tracy watched the two men, her mind caught in a tangle of thought. Who was Jon? As far as she knew detectives didn't make enough money to buy into a business such as Davy's. The more she looked, the more confused she became. And by the time they left the Hawk's Nest and moved on to the rest of the evening she was no closer to an answer.

The kiss that had reached into her being and pulled forth responses she'd thought were sleeping hadn't been a preview of coming events. Jon left her at her door with a kiss that held more sweetness than passion and a promise to call her sometime the next day. Tracy went to bed, not sure whether she was glad or sorry he hadn't continued what he'd started. She did know she would see him again.

Chapter 5

An alarm buzzed. Jon grunted, rolled onto his back and slapped the clock silent. He could not afford any more sleepless nights. One of the first lessons he had learned as a rookie was to make use of every available opportunity to rest. There had been days when he would have given his best shirt for an extra hour of sleep. So what was he doing lying awake most of the night thinking about Tracy Michaels? When he had drifted off for a bit, insult had been added to injury with dreams that would have gotten him arrested. A faint grin lifted his lips at the memory of one of the more vivid fantasies.

The phone rang, disturbing his enjoyable, but useless, pastime.

"Roger? What the devil do you want at this hour? You should still be nursing that cold."

Roger wasn't in the mood to appreciate the reminder. "I couldn't stay in bed any longer. I can think of a lot of uses for a bedroom but being sick isn't one of them. I've been sitting here thinking. I want to run a check on the employee records of those burned-out businesses again. We should get the social security numbers checked if no one else has, present addresses, past, the works. It's just possible someone missed something down the line." He paused to cough and then swear irritably. "Much as I hate it, about all I'm good for at the moment anyway is paperwork."

Pushing himself out of bed, Jon stood naked. The sunlight filtering through the Bahama blinds on the windows highlighted taut muscles and smooth flesh. Jon controlled a sympathetic grin at Roger's disgusted tone. One thing his partner wasn't good at was sitting in one place for long. "Sounds good to me. We haven't got anything to lose at this point."

After giving Roger a short update on the progress of the case so far, Jon replaced the receiver and headed for the bathroom. A shower and three cups of coffee, two eggs and a slice of toast set him up for the day. The radio played as he cooked and later washed up before leaving his apartment. He wondered if Tracy was at the radio station already. Was she an early riser? Did she eat breakfast or was she one of those women permanently on a diet? She had certainly enjoyed her dinner the night before, relishing each bite with true appreciation. And that white chocolate cake she had ordered was not the kind of thing eaten by a woman who worried about adding pounds to her beautiful body. Getting into his car, he decided to try to make a date with her for lunch. He needed something to look forward to if he was going to have to listen to Roger grumble while they retraced some steps in the investigation.

Tracy finished the schedule for the late-afternoon show she produced and laid down her pen. She still had to type the format, which was her least favorite task of the many that fell under the heading of producer. She glanced at her watch and grimaced. Twenty minutes to airtime of her own show. The flutter of nerves in her stomach was uncharacteristic, but it seemed as if it were a permanent fixture in her life for now. She was torn between nervousness and the hope that Bo would call again. Although she believed from both a personal and a professional standpoint in helping whenever and wherever possible, she didn't mind admitting to herself that Bo made her very uneasy. There was a tone in his voice that bordered on personal—*too* personal. Without Jon's strength and expertise she would have had severe reservations about encouraging the line the station had taken.

She leaned back in her chair, knowing she should be typing that schedule and knowing she wouldn't. Jon had been on her mind since she had awakened this morning. She had thought of him while she bathed, wondering if he were up and what his morning ritual was. Did he sleep on the right or the left side of the bed? Did he wear pajamas? She had never daydreamed about a man before; even Lee hadn't prompted such curiosity. Trying to tell herself that she was fascinated by both Jon's unusual occupation and the seeming paradox in his nature was useless. And writing off her curiosity to physical chemistry wasn't

enough, either. It was more than that. She liked his
mind, she realized with a faint smile. He intrigued her
when she had thought herself past being intrigued by
anything.

The phone rang. She reached for it without thinking.

"Tracy?" Jon relaxed in his chair, propping his feet
on his desk. Roger was muttering in the background
but he ignored the noise.

Tracy straightened, a smile on her lips. "Jon. To
what do I owe this call?"

"Hunger." The word slipped out before he could
stop it. "As in lunch," he added hastily.

Tracy licked her lips, glad he wasn't near. The last
thing she wanted him to see was the flush on her face
or the way she had reacted to that one word. "Today?" It was a wonder the word came out without a
quiver.

"Definitely. Do you know Gerard's?"

"Yes." The restaurant was quiet, intimate and ex-
pensive. Once again, she wondered about Jon's source
of income.

"Twelve?"

"Easily."

"If I'm late don't be angry. My schedule has a way
of getting snarled at the worse possible moments. If
I'm more than ten minutes overdue eat without me
and I'll make it up to you later."

Touched but amused, too, at the way he explained
his work, Tracy asked, "Do you always invite a
woman out on one hand and lay down a list of excuses on the other?" Despite the fact that she had been

thinking about him she was a little surprised at her deliberate attempt to extend the call.

"I never have before, at least not before the situation arose." He shifted in his chair, startled that he had changed his pattern for Tracy. He hadn't thought about his excuse; he'd only responded to the need to prepare her in case he was delayed.

"Oh." Tracy wished she hadn't brought the subject up. She had meant to tease him, not get into deep water.

Jon turned his head as a particularly nasty oath from Roger caught his attention. The interruption gave him the breather he needed to get back on track. "I've got to go. See you at twelve. I'll be listening to the show." No one expected Bo to be back on the phone today, but no plan had presented itself to draw the man out.

"I'm nervous." She didn't know what had prompted her to confide her unease, but she didn't regret the words.

He frowned because he hadn't expected that reaction. "Neither Doc nor I think you're in any danger at this point. We have the wire-tap people setting up today. Is there something specific bothering you or is the feeling just general?" He hated the calm neutrality of his voice but he had to know.

"I'm not holding anything back about the case."

He heard her silent plea, whether she meant him to or not. "I can come over. Give me ten minutes."

"No. Stay there. I'm all right. Besides, I'd feel the fool. As you say there's no danger." The bad feelings that she'd had since she'd last talked to Bo were intensifying. Maybe she was calling upon the well-developed survival instincts that women had honed since the time when men stalked their mates. But she couldn't bring herself to tell Jon that she was positive she had a reason for worrying.

"You're sure?"

"Yes. And now I've got to go. Five minutes to air."

Jon sat for a moment after Tracy had hung up, listening to the dial tone in his ear. He worked on hunches, instinct and intuition in whatever case he was solving. This one had a bad feel to it. On the surface it should have been an ordinary arson case. Yet the more they dug into it the more he became convinced large pieces of the puzzle were missing. He had a feeling Tracy felt the same way he did, although he knew she wouldn't admit it. It hadn't taken ten minutes in her company to realize the lady didn't believe in things she couldn't taste, touch or hold. She was a Realist with a capital *R*.

"Jon, damn it, don't sit there daydreaming about that woman while I bust my tail doing donkey work. Take one of these reports and get moving on it. I'm coming up empty. So far all the addresses of the partial list of employees seem to check out, and I've just got the list of their social security numbers. For some fool reason they weren't included in the original report. You'd assume that's the first thing any thinking person would look at to sort through suspects. A person only gets one legitimate number and every employer has to ask for it if he's on the up-and-up—as all the businesses are in this case."

Jon took the report with a grin. Much to Roger's disgust, he reached over to turn on the radio the chief had placed on his desk this morning. "Quit grumbling. You're going to give yourself an ulcer to go with that cold. The chances are someone did check, and that's why the list is misplaced. Running down those numbers and verifying the people they belong to would take time even with the help of computers. So close your mouth so I can hear Tracy's show."

Roger glanced up from the sheet he was scowling at. "You think that creep is going to call in today?"

Jon sobered and shrugged. "I wouldn't think so. I just wish we'd been able to get the judge to agree to a tap on the call-in lines."

"I hate this nit-picking junk of the legal system. Give me the good old days when the sheriff shot it out in the street with the bad guys. I hate paperwork and letter-of-the-law judges. And I'm so fed up with going through here-today-gone-tomorrow employees, I could spit."

Jon laughed aloud at the image, one of Roger's more toned-down ones. Although privately, in some ways, he agreed with Roger, he wasn't about to admit it. "Well, not in here. The city council is on that improve-the-class-of-a-police-station kick."

"Yeah, and we all know it's a crock. You ever heard of a classy station? The crooks don't care, and we're too damn busy to notice."

Jon waved Roger to silence as he leaned forward to catch Tracy's greeting to her listening audience.

Tracy glanced at the clock on the control room wall. Five more minutes until sign-off. It looked as if Jon was right. Bo wouldn't be calling today. None of the names on the monitor before her even vaguely resembled his. The way the phones had been ringing, he had to be the only person in Palm Beach County who wasn't trying to get through. She fielded the next-to-the-last caller. Maybe Bo couldn't get through. They had done their best to keep one line free in case he did try to make contact, but even that was lit now. Sighing soundlessly, she pushed the final button.

"Good morning, Tracy, this is Bo again."

The quiet words, softly spoken in that distorted voice, put a sparkle in Tracy's eyes even as a chill passed over her body. "Hi, Bo. You called in yesterday, didn't you?"

"You remember." His pleasure was unmistakable.

Tracy shivered again. She wasn't imagining his intimate tone. "You had an interesting viewpoint," she explained automatically, her mind racing with possibilities. Jon had explained all the legal reasons they couldn't trace the call on the public lines. Her job was simply to keep Bo talking, strengthening the contact he seemed intent on fostering, perhaps prompting him to make contact in the future on one of the private lines to the station. She didn't like the assignment, but she intended to do her best.

"Your audience doesn't think so. They think the firebug should be put away. Do you think so?"

Oh, boy, how did she answer that one? Tracy thought fast. As a host her course was clear and would probably mean the end to the contact. As a person who might be able to give the police a thread to hang on to, she had to keep him talking and receptive.

"I don't know enough of the circumstances to say." The silence went on so long she thought she had lost him, until she heard a sigh.

"You're the only one who thinks like that. I had forgotten how kind and sympathetic Virginians could be. Thank you."

At the click of the broken connection in her ear, Tracy stared at the light in front of her, watching it blink off. She took her cue to end the show without thinking about it. What had he meant that he had forgotten how sympathetic and kind Virginians could be?

"What the devil did he mean by that remark?" Roger demanded, glaring at the radio as though it was its fault that he didn't have an answer.

"How would I know?" Jon shot back irritably. They had made a serious error in judgment. Tracy was the draw, not her show's subject matter. "That guy talks to Tracy as if he knows her."

"Then let's run another check on her. Maybe there's a Bo somebody in her background."

As a detective, Jon should have jumped at the chance of possible connection. As a man he didn't want Tracy any more involved than she already was. "That's not what I meant. Besides, that remark about Virginia could simply mean that they're both from the same state. It doesn't have to be a personal connection at all."

"Don't fight over peanuts. We need a solid lead, something besides a phone connection made at this Bo's instigation or whim."

"I'm meeting her for lunch. I'll tell her then."

Roger read the purpose in his expression. "We don't have to have her agree to make that check."

"Any rookie knows that," Jon murmured.

"I knew that woman was trouble." Roger got to his feet, jamming the report he still hadn't finished with into the desk drawer. "I'm going to lunch, and when I get back I'm calling the social security office. There must be some way they can cross-reference the burned-out businesses and maybe help us get a more complete list of employees to augment the lost records of each company. All the regulars that everyone remembers check out. I think you were right this morning when you said the firebug was probably a temporary employee, probably someone who blended into the woodwork so well no one recalls him."

"Are you sure you don't know this guy?" Jasper demanded, pacing his office, stopping only to stare at Tracy.

"For the third time I do not know the man. There's something familiar about his voice but I can't place it with a face and I'm sure I would be able to if I knew him, in spite of the distortion," Tracy said, spacing her words as though she were talking to a particularly dense person.

"Do you have any ideas about why he's singling you out? Hunches? Anything?"

"I wish I did. The only think I can think is that he's either from Virginia or he lived there long enough to have caught my old show. There is something about the way he says certain words," she said thoughtfully.

Jasper threw himself into his chair, scowling at Tracy. "I don't like this. You're beginning to remind me of a sitting duck in front of a hunter's blind. I don't like the feeling one bit. Boosting the ratings and getting involved for civic reasons is acceptable, but I won't have you or anyone at this station in danger.''

"We aren't even sure this guy and the firebug are the same person."

"The evidence isn't in, I'll agree. But I think this is our guy."

He stopped, watching her as though he expected her to argue.

"You might be right. But what alternative do we have? Right now, I seem to be the only link. Like it or not, I'm staying."

Jasper's scowl deepened. "What's on the agenda tomorrow?"

"The school thing. I doubt we can gain any more, pushing this issue right now. For one thing it will look too fishy. Jon said we would play it by ear."

"The guy may go cold on us."

Tracy wasn't sure how she felt about backing off. "Or he may do what he did today and keep calling in, regardless of the topic."

Jasper blinked like a startled owl. "That doesn't make sense."

"Does any of this?" Tracy collected her handbag from the chair and headed for the door. "Now if you're done with me, I have a date for lunch and if I don't hurry I'm going to be late."

Tracy entered the restaurant. The air-conditioning inside made a sharp contrast to the humid Florida heat outside. The maître d' greeted her by name, startling her.

"If you will come this way. Mr. Kent is waiting."

Tracy followed the man, her eyes alight with a curiosity that she meant to satisfy. Maître d's did not bow to just anyone.

Jon watched her walk toward him, liking the way she moved. Many women swayed, their stride a subtle, and sometimes not so subtle, invitation to the male. Tracy glided, looking as though she knew some special law of nature that the rest of her kind did not. Grace. That was it. In an age where grace and ease of manner were not characteristics sought after, she epitomized both.

"You made it, I see," Tracy murmured as she took her seat. The windows at Jon's back were covered in reflective sun film, giving a muted but beautiful view of the intracoastal.

"Just barely. The chief stopped me on the way out the door." He paused to allow Tracy to give her drink order to the waiter. "He's angry that we miscalculated on Bo's linkup with your show." There was no easy way to tell her the conclusions they had drawn so he didn't try. "Doc and all of us agree it isn't the topic that has his eye as much as either you or your show."

Tracy inclined her head, having come to the same realization. "Jasper collared me, too, and he was in no better frame of mind than your boss. For a while he was even of the opinion that I might know the guy."

Concerned, Jon asked, "Did he give you trouble about it?"

Tracy relaxed, surprised that she had been worried that Jon would share that opinion. "No. He asked, and I told him that I felt certain I didn't know the man. No problem." Tracy smiled at the waiter as he placed a glass of white wine before her and then took their orders. When they were alone again, she continued. "There is something about this guy that seems familiar. If he weren't so careful to disguise his voice I might be able to make the connection, but as it is..." She shrugged slightly as her words trailed off.

Jon frowned, turning the idea over in his mind. "Is it his voice or the man himself?"

"I'm almost sure it's his voice. There's something about the way he says certain words that makes me think he might be from my home state." She shrugged awkwardly. "I don't know. Maybe I'm imagining things."

Jon studied her, seeing more than he thought she wished him to know. Sharing didn't seem to come easily to her. She was wary when he had given her no reason to be. "I don't think you're a woman who imagines things," he murmured.

"I'm not usually. I also don't act like a nervous rabbit, either," she admitted.

Jon studied her in surprise. "I never thought you were. In fact you strike me as a very self-sufficient person, someone who doesn't run for help or cover at the first sign of trouble. I like that."

Tracy smiled slightly, acknowledging the compliment. She forgot the firebug for the moment to concentrate on Jon. "And you're easy to talk to but I think you know that. Actually, I think you work at it."

"Meaning?" Jon met her eyes. He knew his own eyes were calm, and revealed nothing of his thoughts. His work had taught him caution, his nature demanded it.

Tracy leaned back in her seat and took a sip of wine before she spoke. "Just who are you? You seem to know a lot of people, and I don't think I've ever been around a man who could command the kind of service in restaurants that you do."

"Why do you want to know?"

She should have known she couldn't ask Jon a question without getting asked one in return. She couldn't give him the real reason—that going forward and giving in to their growing attraction was impossible until she could know and trust him. As long as there were blank spaces in his life, she was afraid. This fear wasn't an emotion she wanted to admit even to herself, but it was one she could not deny.

"Unlike you, I don't like all puzzles, especially not ones that might affect me personally. Your pieces don't match. I need to understand why." Pleased with herself for the sudden inspiration, Tracy drank her wine and waited.

Jon hesitated, caught by her honesty and not sure how to deal with it. "So I'm to satisfy your curiosity?"

Put like that, her demand sounded selfish and intrusive. She watched him, seeing the immovable quality in his expression that said something of the man. He would not yield to a halfway answer. Games were not his style unless he was in the mood to play. And apparently with her, he was not. The knowledge could have frightened her; instead, it was reassuring.

"I need to know."

The reply was soft. If Jon had not been listening closely he would have missed her words, yet there was no way to deny their impact. His past was just that. His. He didn't share it lightly or with many. Only Sam, Roger and one or two others knew of it.

"There isn't all that much to tell." He hesitated, amazed to realize that he was intending to let her into this part of his life. "My father owned a little restaurant in Chicago. He and Mom loved the place, and it supported our family fairly well. My three brothers and I worked there after school. It wasn't the best neighborhood, but in the early days it didn't matter. Then things started to go downhill. Pop lost customers. The good life frayed around the edges. Street gangs started taking over the area and my youngest brother joined one. Pop found out and took after him and brought him home for good. The gang was furious at having their power shown up to be so small. They came into the restaurant late one night. Pop and Mom were the only ones there." Jon paused, staring into space, forgetting where he now was as he relived that night.

"They trashed the place and beat my father up. He had a heart attack on the way to the hospital and died. Mom sold what little was left and moved from the only home she had ever known because she was afraid something else bad would happen."

Tracy reached across the table to cover his hand with hers. "Jon, I'm so sorry. Why didn't you tell me to mind my own business?"

Jon looked into her eyes and wondered the same thing himself. Ignoring the question he couldn't answer, he finished his story. "The story has a nice ending. My brothers and I helped Mom start another restaurant with the proceeds from the old place plus Pop's life insurance, this time in Tampa, where we had moved. It was a smashing success. My oldest brother runs it now that Mom is gone. The money he paid me to buy out my share of the place gave me the idea to invest in an eatery here as a silent partner. One turned into three.'' He turned her hand in his, staring for a moment at the smooth palm. ''I keep my fingers in the restaurant business because I love it and it reminds me of home and family, plus it provides an extra source of income. My work isn't the best paid in the world.''

''But why become a cop if you like restaurants so much?''

''To make a difference.'' He met her eyes. ''I know what being a victim is about. No one should be at the mercy of another person. I can't remake the world, but I can do my part to make a corner of it cleaner.'' He shrugged. ''Besides, I told you I also like the challenge of the job.''

''You'll have to admit, it is a strange combination of occupations.''

''No stranger than a woman who buys a run-down house in a jungle and sets out to restore it herself. Or one who owns the ugliest dog that was ever born and calls him Handsome. Or one who makes her living in a medium that probably gets overlooked as a career choice in this high-tech era of videos, televisions and instant visual stimulation.''

She laughed at the description of her life. ''Put like that, it sounds as if I need my head examined.''

''Why? Because you don't do things the ordinary way? I like that. You must, too, or you wouldn't do the things you do. Why worry? Enjoy. There are enough things in this life that we have to fight for. Don't waste your energy on worrying about the things that should be a pleasure.''

"An interesting philosophy." The warmth of his grasp called to her. She wanted more. The look in his eyes was intense, a contradiction to the soothing flow of words on his lips.

"But then we've established I'm a bit of a strange detective."

For the first time, Tracy could hear a trace of his Northern accent. She smiled, realizing she had been given a rare gift. She might not fully trust Jon, but he had trusted her with something very special.

"Does anyone else know about your background?" Impulse prompted the question.

"Besides my own family, only you, Roger and Sam." His fingers tightened on hers. He could not help but hope she would feel safer with him now that she knew something the rest of the world did not.

Tracy's smile died. She hadn't expected his answer. She looked down at their linked hands, unable to bear the intensity of his eyes. She had given Jon honesty, but she had withheld her trust. Her lack of trust seemed so unfair now. Jon could have evaded her and she wouldn't have known the difference. She was being drawn more closely to him with each day. Since he had given her his past, she owed him her own. The thought frightened her. What would he think of her when he knew? She raised her head, looking for the answers on his face. Curiosity and a strange kind of tenderness were unexpected.

"If you feel I'm trying to pressure you because of what I told you, don't. I didn't do it for that reason. I won't ask questions of you. You can tell me anything but I won't ask."

Without realizing it, Tracy's hands tightened around his. For the moment she was grateful for his understanding. Later she would wonder why it was easy for him to give. "How did you know?"

"I learned how to read faces a long time ago and I've had years of practice. Right now your face is talking to me even though *you* won't." He smiled at her, wanting to see the pain and suffering in her eyes gone. "Don't worry so. I don't believe in force or taking what isn't mine to have. You're safe." He leaned back in his chair, releasing her hand so that the waiter could serve them.

Tracy felt the absence of warmth and strength the moment he let her go. She wanted to grab his hand back and hold on tight. She had stood alone for most of her life. Only with Lee had she offered even a piece of herself, and then she had found betrayal and lies. Jon walked in honesty, accepting life rather than turning cynical as his partner had. He touched her and she forgot all the reasons to be cautious. She learned the meaning of wanting and needing something she was afraid to take. She had never called herself a coward until she met Jon.

Chapter 6

"Bingo." Roger tossed a sheet of paper down on Jon's desk before leaning against the corner and folding his arms across his chest. "Your meticulous personality must be rubbing off on me. Take a look at that. I've almost got a complete list of every employee and his social security number from each of the burned-out businesses in this town. With most of the records torched that was a job in itself. The fire marshal's office did have a lot of them, though, and the social security office was able to do a cross-reference check to fill in any blanks. While I was at it, I tried to run down the state and/or town of origin for the issuing of the numbers. I've got ninety-nine percent of the data. And guess what I've found?"

"I'm listening." Jon studied the sheet before him.

"I also put in a call to a friend of mine in Washington."

"Female, no doubt," Jon murmured without looking up.

Roger shrugged. "The lady is a cousin of an old college friend. The point is, she's also been doing some cross-checking, using the destroyed businesses as reference points. She's come up with a few names that we didn't have—people who are no longer employed with the companies. One of the cases turned up something interesting. A temporary man with an incorrect social security number—one that doesn't match his name." He propped one hip on the edge of the desk. "We're checking further into the guy's work history now."

"The number could be the result of a typo." Jon stared at the name circled on the list in front of him. "Bob Little. Bo? Bob?"

"Maybe." Roger crossed his arms and frowned. "Anyway, I also sent for Orlando's workups and Jacksonville's. They should be here this afternoon. If they haven't got this much in-depth info on employees, I'll do it myself. If this guy shows up again we might have the link we've been looking for."

"Get somebody to help you. Sam has okayed as much manpower as we can beg, borrow or steal. Also go back say five years if you can. See if there are any duplicate names that crop up, same person or a mother, brother, sister, lover, wife."

The look in Roger's eyes sharpened. "What are you getting at?"

"Right now I'm operating on the assumption that Bo is the firebug and not just some nut looking for attention by getting involved with a high-visibility crime. I keep remembering his comment about justice. I think he got himself a job at some time in every one

of these places and for some reason feels he or someone he cares about was mistreated. Right now that's
the only theory that makes sense. Up until now every
one has been operating on the idea that this guy just
likes to watch things burn. I don't think that's true.''

"Your hunches are rarely wrong, and this one
sounds better than anything else I've heard. Let's go
with it." Roger collected his research and hurried from
the room.

Bo sat under the tree, the water behind him lapping
gently at the bulkhead that protected Flagler Drive
from being washed into the intracoastal. Tracy's car
was there. He knew it was hers because he had
watched her arrive this morning. She was prettier than
her picture. Just being near her made home seem a
little closer, his life a little less lonely. She had smiled
at one of her co-workers, and he had wished she would
smile at him. It had been so long since he was happy.
But he couldn't rest. He couldn't think of himself, he
reminded himself irritably. Justice had to be served.

The door opened. He watched the cluster of people
emerging from the radio station stop on the steps to
chat for a moment. He recognized Tracy immediately
as she stood talking to a petite redhead. He stayed still,
watching.

Soon. The end was almost here. Yes, she was the
one to trust. She would not betray him.

Tracy shifted restlessly, feeling nervous without
knowing why. Aside from Bo's phone call, nothing
about the day had been out of the ordinary. Yet for the

past two hours she had felt as if something was out of sync.

"What's wrong?" Nikki asked, looking concerned.

"I don't know. Did you ever get the feeling that something was happening right under your nose and you should know about it? Since this firebug thing, I've discovered I have nerves I didn't know existed." She laughed a little unsteadily. "I don't usually jump at shadows."

"For what it's worth, I don't think you are jumping at shadows. I've got the feeling that someone is staring at us or watching the station or something. One of the files I needed had slipped out of the stack I took home last night. So I had to come out to my car a while ago. I spent most of the time looking over my shoulder. It was a weird feeling." Nikki glanced around.

Tracy hadn't wanted Nikki to reinforce her suspicions. "With two of us getting the feeling, I don't think we can afford to ignore the problem. I guess I'd better tell Jon."

Nikki looked interested, forgetting her unease in the face of this new development. "Are you seeing him again tonight?"

There was no point in hiding the truth. "For dinner. I'm cooking, or at least I'd planned to until our meeting ran overtime."

"You shouldn't be standing here. If it were me, and Roger were the man I was cooking for, I'd be hotfooting it home." Nikki grinned, then added, "I'd pick out the sexiest thing in my closet and give myself a bubble bath."

Tracy laughed softly, for a moment forgetting her tension to tease her friend. "To hear you talk anyone would think you were an aggressive, take-what-you-want-when-you-want-it female. We both know that isn't so."

"You're trying to change the subject. I asked about Jon and you. Not for a reading of my character."

Tracy sighed, knowing that she should have realized she wouldn't get away so easily. "I don't know what you want me to say. I find the man interesting, despite my better judgment about getting involved at this stage of my life and in these circumstances. I like him. He makes me feel good." She smiled faintly. "He makes me feel like a woman again—new, fresh, clean. I'm forgetting about Lee and I thought I never would," she admitted finally.

Nikki's eyes conveyed her understanding and sympathy. "Then hurray for Jon Kent. It's about time you had some fun out of life. I like the man, too. So go for it." She turned to open the door of her car. "I can't wait to hear the next installment."

"You're treading on thin ice, my friend," Tracy warned, trying not to laugh.

"Not in Florida I'm not. Besides, I took all the self-defense courses." She waved as she started the motor then drove away.

Tracy stood for a moment staring after her, thinking about Nikki's last words. Nikki was in many ways her antithesis. Nikki liked being single, took pains to make sure that she was completely self-sufficient. Tracy liked being independent, but she didn't want to spend the rest of her life alone. Lee had shaken her confidence badly, but she still believed in loving and home and children and forever. Having someone to protect her, to stand beside her when she needed support, to hold her when she needed comfort and to touch her when she needed love. Having someone of her own to worry over, to cook for, to love with and fight with. She wanted it more than a place, more than a partnership, more than a satisfying career. She had desired it all and had been intending to achieve each of her carefully chosen goals. That was why it was so important to her to buy a house and turn it into a home. She needed that security for when she moved to the next step of bringing a man into her life again. Then Jon had happened. Her wonderful timetable had been shaken, until nothing was as she had planned. Still, she couldn't make herself regret letting him into her life. She didn't know where she was going anymore, but even that was losing its importance. For the first time since Lee she was heading into the future without a cautiously set course, risking herself and the peace she had created.

Bo watched her smile, saw the sun gleam in her hair and remembered another time and place. He remembered happiness like a half-forgotten dream. In his hell, in being the hunted, he had found an angel and memories of a time he would never know again. For one brief moment he felt regret. Then another memory came, a nightmare this time. A face, a voice. The pain of not being there for the one who meant so much to him. He blinked, focusing on Tracy as she got in her car. She didn't know how he hurt. She was all smiles and grace. He wanted her to know there was a reason. He wanted her to understand so that all the guilty would know their part in his nightmare. His hands clenched at his sides. Three more and then he was done.

Jon hurried into his shower, cursing the paper search that had turned up a few clues but had made him late for his date with Tracy. He wasn't accustomed to worrying about being on time, especially because he'd explained the demands of his work. After drying off he pulled on dark slacks, a pale-blue-striped shirt and no tie. After he donned a pair of loafers he was on his way. Popping the portable blue light on the top of his car, he broke one of his own rules and used the emergency warning to speed through the streets to Tracy's house. He arrived seven minutes late and not feeling a bit guilty for the tactic that had gotten him there so quickly. Tracy was waiting for him on the front porch, her ugly mutt standing guard at her side.

"That was some arrival," Tracy murmured, smiling as she watched him come toward her. His easy stride, a lazy walk that covered ground with deceptive ease, never varied.

"I don't like being late if I can help it." He shrugged, not prepared to make more of an explanation. Bending, he brushed her lips, intending only to take a taste. But he found himself caught by her scent. Without thought he deepened the kiss, his tongue stroking hers as she leaned into him. Her groan built the heat in his blood. His hands tightened on her shoulders, drawing her nearer.

It was becoming harder to remember all the reasons why he shouldn't allow himself to become involved with Tracy. He didn't like needing her, wanting her smiles, her touch and her body close to his. An affair could be physically intense, but he should be safe from the emotional ties that were beginning to form around him. He was caring too much. He should back off but couldn't make himself do it.

Until he touched her, Tracy hadn't been sure what she would do. His mouth on hers unleashed the need to yield. She leaned into him, her arms slipping around his body to pull him closer. His returning embrace was swift and sure, and felt as though they had been lovers before. She gasped softly as he tilted her hips to cradle him. His tongue played with hers, answering her need with undisguised hunger that was hot, sweet and pure male. His scent clung to her, his taste was on her lips, his touch was the breath of fire on her skin.

"Do you know what you're doing?" he asked, lifting his head to stare into her eyes.

"Probably not," she admitted, her breathing rougher than she would have liked. "This is new to me." Honesty shouldn't have been so easy or so necessary.

"Me, too." His fingers traced the curve of her lips.

"It doesn't feel as if it's new to you." A foolish remark but one determined to be said. She waited, needing something more than she understood.

"Reaction to you. I'm not like the man who hurt you. I don't play games. I don't know how and I never wanted to learn."

Tracy froze, not expecting him to see what she had tried to hide. "How did you know?"

The truth was he had done his research. He chose to tell her a gentle lie to spare her pride. "You go still in-

side every time I come near you. Animals do that in
the wild when they're threatened. I know I've done
nothing to trigger that kind of response. It has to be
someone else.'' He stroked her back, seeking the tension in her muscles, angered that their passion could
be so easily overshadowed by a memory.

Tracy wanted to lay her head on his shoulder and
tell him everything. But the caution her involvement
with Lee had taught her got in the way. ''It isn't you.''
She couldn't give him much but she could give him
that.

''Then who? I can't believe this guy is here. I think
you left him in Virginia.'' He probed carefully, wanting her to trust him enough to share her past, as he had
given her his.

''I did.'' She closed her eyes, realizing Jon would
not leave the question unanswered. Trying to divert his
attention, she murmured, ''Let's go in so I can start
dinner. I was late getting off work today.''

He felt her resistance and fought the need to demand the truth. He couldn't fight an enemy he
couldn't identify. Having the facts regarding her past
relationship was not enough, but he had no right to
push her. Physically she wanted him but emotionally
she needed an out. Logic told him he should have been
pleased that she could demand no more of him than
she was prepared to give, but he was hurt nonethe-
less. He released her and stepped back.

''You're right.''

Tracy opened her eyes and wished she hadn't. He
was wearing that closed expression that gave away
none of his thoughts. ''Don't shut me out.'' The words
escaped, surprising them both.

Jon's brows rose as he studied her. The distress on her face was plain to see. "I think the shoe is on the other foot," he murmured. He was getting in deeper with every word he spoke, and yet he couldn't stop himself. He wanted to know her secrets. He wanted her total trust, not just the pieces she offered like precious gold.

Tracy spread her hands, wondering how she could explain. "I'm trying."

"Why do you have to try? At least tell me that much."

She glanced away, seeing the home she was building, the new life she had begun to carve for herself. "Not now."

"When?"

Anger rode him, spurs in his patience. He reined in, fighting himself and the passion she could ignite with just a look. Of all the women in his world, it had to be this one who had gotten past his defenses. He was no more anxious than she to become a part of a pair. His job demanded his concentration. His conscience would not allow him to enter into a commitment when he could offer less than the whole of himself. Tracy was different. She made him want things. She made him think one way and react another. His careful, methodical existence was shot, and he didn't care. He wanted her. More than that, he wanted her to want him with the same lack of logic.

"Give me time."

"How much?"

"How do I know?"

She looked back at him then to see a tall, strong man who might bend but not bow. Would he understand the battering her pride had taken? Would Jon see what Lee's betrayal had done to her ability to believe in her own judgment? Would he see that she couldn't rush headlong into his life without understanding where they were going and how they would get there?

Never had patience been so hard to deliver. "All right. I'll back off if that's what you want. But I'm no saint. Don't respond to me as if you're ready to come to me and then expect me to walk away. I won't do it the next time. I want you more than I've ever wanted anyone. By necessity I've learned to be a loner. You make me forget that. I'm no more sure of my ground than you seem to be."

Tracy laughed, a rough sound that carried a hint of tears. "Don't growl at me."

"Honey, I would like to do a lot more, believe me." He glanced down, his lips twisting at the evidence of the fire that burned beyond his control. "I thought I had grown past the age of this."

"You're not alone."

"That's what I keep telling myself, but it isn't helping." He turned and headed down the steps. "Let's go where there are people and noise. As much as I would enjoy having you cook for me, I don't think being alone with you right now would be good for either of us."

Stopping only long enough to put Handsome inside the house and to get her purse, Tracy followed silently. She couldn't argue with his reasoning. She needed something to divert her mind, too.

"Another time." He stopped and looked over his shoulder.

Their eyes met. Both realized the future might bring the confrontation they had avoided tonight. Both knew the price honesty could hold and acknowledged, too, there would be no backing away.

"Another time," she agreed slowly before taking the step that brought her to his side.

He held out his hand. She placed hers in it. His smile was slight but visible. She relaxed. For now it was enough to share the night.

Bo watched from the shadows, scowling at the pair. She had let that man touch her. Who was he? Was he important to her? Her lover? A friend? He hadn't missed the blue light on the unmarked car when it arrived. The man touched Tracy as though she belonged to him, and yet he seemed to be a cop. Bo decided he had to know as he felt the hate build within him when they kissed. The porch light shone on the man who held Tracy in his arms. He would remember the face.

He watched Tracy put her hand in the man's, saw her smile. Her voice was soft with caring. Suddenly, his fists clenched as the dying sun touched the liquid traces of her tears. The man had made her cry. Hate turned to rage, a need to get revenge. That man would pay for hurting her. Bo had learned how to make those pay who went through life taking rather than giving.

Tracy shivered as she slipped into the car seat. The feeling of being stalked was back again. Jon frowned as he held the door. "Are you cold?"

Tracy looked uneasily out the window, seeing nothing but the beginning of the night to come. The shadows were deepening with each passing minute. *Hiding places*. The phrase slid into her mind, bringing another shudder. Wrapping her hands around her arms, she tried to fight her imagination.

"No." She knew before she saw his eyes narrow that she'd been too quick with that answer.

Jon shut the door and glanced around casually as he walked to the driver's side. Tracy was nervous and trying to hide it. He hadn't missed the way Handsome hadn't left her side until the dog identified him. He also hadn't missed her searching look just now. He started the car without speaking, although his attention was focused on her rather than his driving. Her sigh of relief was soundless but visible.

"Want to tell me about it?"

Tracy started, her gaze sliding to his then away. "I don't know what you're talking about." This all had to be her imagination, no matter what Nikki said.

He exhaled deeply, irritated that she wouldn't trust him. "We both know better." He waited. "Something has you jumping at your own shadow. Even your dog feels it. What is it?"

She shouldn't have been glad he was backing her into a corner. She should have been fighting him. All the "should haves" in the world couldn't stop the relief easing over her at his probing. "You'll think I'm paranoid."

"Try me." He glanced at her, taking in the pallor that washed the passion and life from her skin.

"I think someone is watching me, but I can't prove it." She would have preferred a less dramatic statement but she was fresh out of ideas.

"Since when?"

His calm question made the explanation easier than it could have been. "Today is the first time I've had the feeling so strongly. I thought it was because the calls from Bo were—and still are—making me nervous. But even Nikki feels the same. I tried telling myself it was my imagination, but I can't make myself believe it."

Jon stared straight ahead, sifting through the possibilities. There weren't that many, and none was reassuring. There was an outside chance that the person watching her wasn't Bo, but Jon wouldn't have bet money on the odds. How had Bo gotten Tracy's address? Had he simply followed her home? And why was he following her? "Why do you link the calls and the feelings together? Instinct or something solid?" He kept his voice calm, not wanting to increase her uneasiness more than was necessary.

"I don't know. That was the best I could do. How can I feel this person at work and here—unless he followed me home?" Her skin prickled at the sudden thought. Better to know the devil than to shake hands with him unaware.

He couldn't conceal the possibilities from her for her own sake. Better to be prepared. "Probably as you haven't been in town long enough for your phone number and address to be in the phone directory, though he could call information." He reached across with one hand to cover her clenched fingers. "I'm not going to tell you not to worry because only a fool would treat this matter lightly. But I can tell you that as of now you won't be alone. When I'm not with you someone will be watching over you."

Tracy felt his warmth wrap around her. The security it provided was temptingly addictive. She tried to remember all the reasons she shouldn't lean on him. Every rationale that occurred to her had a general application that did not fit Jon. He wouldn't take advantage of the situation. He would not lie to her.

"I'm glad." She smiled a little, trying to lighten the mood.

Jon exhaled slowly, deeply. He had feared she would push him away. Threading his fingers through hers, he tugged her hand lightly. "I don't suppose you'd like to use that middle seat belt and slide over here next to me."

She laughed softly, relaxing now that she had told him. "Protecting me already?" Unbuckling the belt with her free hand, she made the switch. She wanted to be close and for now she could afford to give in to her wants.

"Our job is to protect and serve. Swore an oath to that." He tucked her head against his shoulder and brushed her lips with his. "You won't let me make love to you yet, so I figure this is the next best thing."

Tracy snuggled closer, allowing the intimacy, enjoying the youthful flavor. "It's been a long time since I did something like this," she admitted, needing to break the silence.

"The same for me." Jon angled his head to steal a kiss.

Tracy met his lips halfway. "I thought we were playing it safe by getting out of the house and around people. I don't think this kind of behavior is what either of us had in mind," she said when he raised his head. "Besides, it could get us in a wreck."

"I like to live dangerously. Want to try for another one?"

"Keep your mind on your driving and your hands on the wheel. I thought policemen obeyed the law."

He laughed, hugging her tight. "Most of the time, unless there's a good reason not to."

"I'm not going to lead with my chin and ask what constitutes a good reason."

"That's what I like. A smart woman and one who knows enough to quit while she's ahead."

Chapter 7

Jon sat down in the chair beside the phone. It was after eleven. The chief wouldn't appreciate being awakened at this hour, but he also wouldn't appreciate not being kept abreast of developments. Jon dialed Sam's number while trying to shake the feeling that Tracy's imagination wasn't playing tricks on her. He'd done his best to persuade her to let him stay the night on her couch, but the lady would have no part of his precaution. According to her, she had the dog, stout locks on the door, and was only minutes from the Jupiter police station. Jon wasn't sure whether it was the explosive chemistry between them, a kind of pride or something in her past that had made her take such a determined stand. The best he could do until Sam could make his precautions official had been to stop by the Jupiter police department and ask the men on patrol to keep an eye on Tracy's house. Despite his arrangements he couldn't relax. But short of camping in his car on her street, an idea that was beginning to seem smarter by the minute, there was nothing else he could do. Silently, he cursed the fishing-village-turned-town that didn't even have streetlights in some of its older sections—one of which was Tracy's.

As the phone kept ringing at Sam's house Jon remembered how hard it had been to restrain Handsome when he was checking over the grounds of Tracy's home. The dog had gone wild at the small grove of trees near the street. Something or someone had used the thicket as a hiding place.

"Yeah, what is it?" Sam's disgruntled voice was rough with sleep.

"It's Jon. We've got a problem."

"It's at moments like this that I wish I'd chosen a different line of work." Despite his complaint there was real interest in his voice. "What kind of a problem?"

"Tracy thinks someone is watching her. If her dog's reaction when I checked over her house before I left was anything to go by, I think she's right."

"You found evidence?"

Jon could almost hear Sam's mind click into high gear. "Not any that would stand up in court. We had a date tonight. She was nervous when I picked her up." Among other things. "I got her talking and she told me she'd been feeling someone was keeping an eye on her around the radio station. Until tonight she had put it down to imagination. She couldn't give me anything to go on. Just feelings."

"Is she the type to let her nerves get the best of her?"

"No." Jon didn't have to think about his reply. "I checked the property and took her dog with me. Monster mutt, nasty teeth and a disposition that would put a wolverine to shame. The dog went nuts when we reached one really secluded spot. I'm sure that was where the watcher had hidden. He would have had a good view of the house. She lives in one of the old sections of Jupiter, right on the water. The property is really overgrown with lots of hiding places and no streetlights. I tried to get her to let me sleep on the couch, but short of forcing the issue I got nowhere. And she wouldn't agree to checking into a hotel for the night. She's got a real thing about that house of hers. No one's going to budge her from it without a bomb. I left her my number and she promised to call if she had a problem. I also stopped at the local station and they've got their patrols keeping a half-hour watch."

"But you're not satisfied. Are you going back there?"

"Yeah. She might have the courage to play sitting duck, but as soon as I got home I realized I don't." Jon ran a hand through his hair. "I think I'm beginning to hate sitting up all night in cars almost as much as you hate answering midnight calls."

"It goes with the territory. I'll make better arrangements in the morning. Until then, use your judgment."

Both men hung up. For now, all that could be done was being done. The next move was Bo's.

One minute Tracy was sleeping peacefully, the next she jerked awake, her heart pounding in fear. Handsome was on his feet, growling low and deep in his throat. The darkness was cold and frightening, although the night was warm. Blinking, she listened, trying to identify the sound that had yanked her out of her dreams with a sick feeling in her stomach. Nothing. Still Handsome growled, as he now paced to the door leading to the hall. He acted as though he wanted to go after something—or someone—but was bound to remain close. Shivering, Tracy thought of every ugly story she'd ever heard about women living alone. She'd been a fool to send Jon home. Her stupid pride had put her in this vulnerable position. If Jon had been here, she wouldn't have been afraid. He would have known exactly what to do.

Anger at herself gave her the strength to move, even though her muscles were almost rigid with the need to stay calm. She eased out of bed and reached for Handsome's collar. Winding her fingers around the leather, she felt less alone, more able to cope. The house was dark as she moved down the hall. She couldn't make herself turn on the lights, although they would have been a comfort in the situation. In some strange way she felt safer in the shadows until she was certain no one else was in the house with her.

The search revealed nothing. Handsome's growls grew softer, finally stopping completely. Whatever had been outside was gone now. Handsome was quiet and calm again.

Tracy needed a cup of herbal tea to settle her nerves so she heated the kettle and tried to think logically.

The house seemed too quiet. Rubbing her arms, she stared at the steam rising from the pot. She'd never get back to sleep now, and she needed to. She had a busy day scheduled at work tomorrow.

Pouring her cup of tea and adding an extra spoon of sugar for good measure, she tried thinking of every boring thing she knew. After two cups of tea and a lot of pacing, she decided she needed some kind of security blanket. Jon. He would listen. He would know what to do. The phone was in her hand without her consciously having made the decision to call. His alert voice was sweet in her ear.

"What's up, honey?" He had just been on his way to his car when he heard the phone ring. Only the feeling that it was Tracy had made him retrace his steps.

Tracy sank onto the bed, tucking her knees under her. The frightening shadows of fear began to recede with his greeting. "I think I'm crying wolf," she murmured shakily, feeling more foolish by the moment.

"Why?" he asked quietly. Tracy sounded as if she were holding back tears.

"Something woke me up. Handsome was growling. We walked through the house but I didn't go outside. He finally calmed down and I've tried to but I can't. I got chicken and called you." The words popped out in a small rush. Tracy paused, took a deep breath and tried for composure. "I shouldn't have."

Jon was prey to two different emotions. His professional side was marking up the incident, fitting it into the picture that was beginning to emerge. The personal side was surprised to realize he was pleased that Tracy had called him instead of one of her friends. He didn't fool himself into thinking her reaction was completely without thought to his work, but he doubted that she would have contacted Roger in the same situation. Bo didn't know it, but he had just done Jon a good turn. Jon's proportions were not meant to be cramped up in a car for hours on end.

"Why don't I come over? I have a foolproof method for putting nervous ladies to sleep."

Tracy shook her head, although the temptation to agree was strong. She didn't want to be alone. She wanted Jon close. "I can't expect you to do that. I'm feeling better, really."

"Well, I'm not. I'm awake, too. I need my own recipe and it takes two. You're the culprit in making me lose sleep, so you'll just have to help me," he said lightly. He didn't want her worrying any more than was necessary. Tracy had been frightened enough for one night. "I'll be there in fifteen minutes. Don't open the door until you're sure it's me."

Bo watched the same car that had come for Tracy earlier roll down the street. He was angry at himself for knocking over the trash can. He should have been more careful. He had frightened her, and he hadn't meant to do that. He'd only wanted to see if she was alone. She had been but she wouldn't be now. It was the cop again. The presence of the man, and his profession, bothered Bo. Had she known him before or had the police latched onto Tracy in an attempt to catch Bo? His anger grew at the thought. They had no right to use her that way.

Jon scanned the area, liking what he saw less with every look. The waterway at the back of the house was dark. Anyone could use it for access. Most of the homes were set back from the road and built far apart from one another. A great deal of shrubbery added to the feeling of seclusion. In the daylight the neighborhood was a piece of country in the center of town. But at night it became a hideaway for anyone who preferred the shadows. At the moment, it looked quiet, peaceful. Jon frowned as he made one more circle of the area. Every vehicle was accounted for, no empty cars were parked at the edge of the street, no person walked on the sidewalk, there wasn't even a dog prowling around.

Finally he pulled into Tracy's yard. The porch light burned brightly as did several lights inside. As he climbed the front steps, Tracy opened the door. She stood framed in the doorway, smiling hesitantly.

"You should have waited until I knocked," he said, taking her arm and easing her inside.

"You said wait until I knew for certain it was you. I did." Actually she had been so anxious for him to arrive she had stood in the dark of the guest room, watching the drive. She had even waited a moment before she had raced for the door.

Jon pulled her into his arms, satisfying his need to hold her without making any demands. "How are you doing now? Any more problems?"

Tracy laid her head against his chest, listening to the steady throb of his heart. The reassuring sound was calming. Her breathing slowed as she relaxed against him. "Handsome has been as quiet as a mouse."

Jon cocked his brow as he looked over her head to the dog sitting on his haunches, watching his every move. A long red tongue slid out as Handsome licked a very impressive set of teeth. "The only thing I can guarantee about that dog's ancestry is the complete lack of mouse blood," he muttered, eyeing Handsome with the same intense stare he was getting from the dog.

"He isn't pretty, but he's smart and he does get the job done."

Jon pressed his cheek to Tracy's hair, pleased to hear her voice smoothing out and her body softening beneath his hands. The tension was easing its grip. "I'll agree to that. Is he trained?" He needed some answers, but no one said he had to alarm her to get them.

"I took him to a friend of mine in Virginia who trained K-9 dogs." Tracy lifted her head to search his expression. "What is it?" she asked quietly. "What is it that you aren't telling me?"

Now that Jon was here she thought she could face anything. No one knew better than she how crazy her growing belief in him was, but she couldn't deny its existence.

"I'm not certain we're dealing with a straight arson problem. This guy has breezed in and hit a few places in three separate cities that we know of. Then he's taken off again. If he were an ordinary arsonist you could attribute his behavior to a fear of being caught. But I don't think that's the reason he's moving around so much. The police are snapping at his heels like a bunch of sharp-toothed terriers. He has no respect for our ability to catch him, so he's getting more brazen and smarter about the fires he sets. He's using a few different methods, but he's shown that he puts a great deal of planning and knowledge in the way he sets up his jobs. And he always makes sure everyone is out of the targets when the fires take place. There's a method to this guy, and it's more than just the thrill of seeing the flames lighting up the sky. Unless the torch is getting paid, he usually stays fairly close to home until he's caught. Nothing in our investigation so far indicates that he's a pro."

"You're talking about motive."

He smiled down at her, his arms tightening around her. "Interested in helping me think this through?"

"Is this your foolproof way of putting me to sleep?"

He shrugged slightly. "It happens. I'm not the most fired-up guy you've ever met, especially when I start one of these mental puzzles. A lot of my work is done with brainpower, not brawn. If there's any glamour in police work, I haven't found it yet. So if you're expecting James Bond-type tales, you won't get them."

For one moment Tracy thought he was teasing—until she looked in his eyes. He actually believed his work was boring, uninteresting to anyone but another cop. "I won't be bored," she said definitely.

Searching her eyes for the truth, he lifted his hand to brush her cheek. Her skin was soft, bare of cosmetics, and he knew he would never forget how she looked in that instant. She didn't find him unexciting, or too involved with his work to make room for her. Her eyes glowed with emotion. Her hair was free and slightly wild about her face. He wanted to laugh as the memories of Amanda complaining about his preoccupation with his work slid into the past—where they belonged.

"Thank you," he murmured, forgetting everything but the feel of her in his arms. He wanted to carry her to the bedroom, lay her down and make sweet love to her until neither of them could remember why he was there.

Tracy raised her hands and framed his face. His eyes were dark, yet filled with a kind of light she could only feel. His body was hard and warm against hers. "I want to explore your mind," she whispered, the unusual words sounding exactly right. "I need to know you. I want to watch you work and see how and why you do what you do. May I?"

"You'll find it tedious for the most part. Not glamorous at all. Most of it is paperwork and fitting pieces that don't seem to match into a pattern that makes sense." This time the truth emerged without any coloring from the past.

"Puzzles."

"Only these are real."

"Share them with me." She glanced at the briefcase he had dropped on the floor when he had taken her in his arms. "Let me help."

To talk to her about the case was one thing; to actually have her offer to pick through the paper facts was something more. He looked into her eyes, hardly daring to believe she meant it. "Because you're involved?"

She didn't pretend to misunderstand. "Maybe, but more." She grinned, suddenly feeling the night settle into place around them. The fear that had brought them together was almost gone. Jon had brought warmth, peace and questions she couldn't wait to explore. Stepping back when she would rather have stayed, she bent and picked up the case.

"Do you need room to spread out? We can use my den. It was one of the bedrooms before I finished with it." She started up the stairs.

Jon watched her walk away, the gentle sway of her hips beneath the thin gown and robe beckoning him to follow. He trailed her up the steps, smiling a little as she started with her questions. He hadn't expected her curiosity about his work. He had become so used to the reactions of the women who had come after Amanda that he was fascinated. Tracy neither found his work a turn-on because of the danger he faced, nor seemed put off by his job's tediousness.

"This is it." Tracy opened the door to the den and walked in. She turned, waiting for Jon's reaction. She realized with a sense of shock that she wanted him to like her home. She had shown her place to no one but Nikki.

Jon glanced around, appreciating the work that must have gone into the remodeling. The real tongue-and-groove paneling was sealed, but not stained, so that the natural color of the wood shone through. Two windows were draped in an open-weave emerald-green linen, which contrasted beautifully with the dusty-green-and-rose Oriental rug on the hardwood floor.

"You like books, too," he murmured, looking over the wall given to filled shelves. Many of the titles were his personal favorites.

Not wanting to reveal how much his obvious pleasure in the room meant to her, Tracy said lightly, "Too much. It's a good thing paperbacks and used bookstores were invented, or I'd be broke by now." She set his case on her desk. "Will this be big enough?"

"Easily. I don't suppose you have some coffee or tea? If we're going to dig into this mess I need fortification. I'll even offer to make it."

She laughed, liking him more with every moment she spent in his company. "You're a nice man, Jon Kent."

Jon grimaced. "I hate that word. I've spent most of my life with that description following me around."

Startled at the bitterness she had unknowingly tripped over, Tracy stared at him. "What's wrong with *nice*?"

"Dogs are nice. Kids are nice. Ice cream is nice. I am not nice. If you want to know the truth, I'm looking at you right now and thinking about things that have nothing to do with your job or mine. You've just had a scare and I want you. That is not the behavior of a *nice* man." He looked at her for a long moment, watching her struggle to respond. Finally, not liking himself for the confession, he turned away to open the briefcase. "Maybe it would be better if you made the coffee or whatever."

Tracy studied his broad back, hurting for him and herself. "I meant it as a compliment. I've never felt good with a man before." One step shortened the distance between them. He tensed but did not face her. "You make me feel safe and comfortable. Is that so wrong?"

"Not wrong but not inspiring, either." He snatched the papers out and slammed them on the desk. He had never been so close to losing his temper.

Irritation flared, blotting out the need to understand and make him understand. "That's a matter of opinion," she returned smartly. "And it's not mine."

Jon turned then, taking in her angry expression and thinking it was the most beautiful thing he had ever seen. He hadn't known how much her opinion mattered to him. It shouldn't have if he was to keep the distance he usually maintained in his relationships. He knew he was coming dangerously close to falling for her, but he couldn't seem to stop himself. More than that he didn't *want* to stop himself. "I guess 'comfortable' and 'safe' are all right."

"You may be good at puzzles but you aren't good at people, at least not me. I don't say what I don't mean. I don't lie and I have no reason to pander to your ego."

He grinned slightly, enjoying her temper even as his own took a nosedive into oblivion. "Actually I'm usually good with people. I just missed with us." He leaned down, risking a lot with a hard, quick kiss. "Sit down and sort through this stuff while I make the coffee, woman. It will give you a chance to read what's there."

Tracy glared at him, reading the satisfaction in his eyes. "I think I've been had."

Jon's grin widened then turned into the full-throated laugh of a man pleased with himself and his world. "Not yet you haven't."

Tracy raised her brows, resisting the urge to laugh with him. "Don't toss out challenges, Kent," she warned, finding her feet in the conversational game.

"Why not? They make good bait for lovely ladies."

"They also make wonderful ways to trip up nice men."

The disputed word became an endearment with the way Tracy drawled it. Jon touched her mouth, his thumb smoothing the lips he had just taken. "Kiss me now and we'll call it a draw," he offered.

Tracy knew she was in over her head. His voice curled around her like an invisible rope and drew her closer. She was one step nearer to joining her life with his, if only for a short time. Did she want to take the final step? She looked into his eyes and saw not love, but rather a need to possess. She could keep running or she could take a chance. Suddenly she was tired of the past having the power to guide her future.

Raising her chin, going on tiptoes, she pulled his head down to hers. "We may both regret this," she whispered as she touched his lips with hers. Nothing in her experience had prepared her for taking the initiative. Lee had always led and she had followed. Jon was a different man. He wanted an equal partner.

Her tongue touched his, expecting an immediate response. His joined hers, repeating the same stroking glide. She leaned against him, letting him take her weight. His hands curved around her shoulders, but he made no move to draw her closer. She probed deeper, seeking the well of passion she knew existed. He matched her move, bringing a groan of need to her lips. Her arms wrapped around him, binding him to her. His body cradled her now, his hips hard and warm against hers.

Jon raised his head, breathing heavily. "Do you mean this?"

Tracy opened her eyes, feeling more a woman than she ever had in her life. He was on fire for her as she was for him. The naked longing on his face was undisguised. "I believe I do," she breathed finally.

"No regrets?"

She shook her head. "None. I want you. I need you." She lifted her lips to his, no longer interested in words.

As he took her mouth, he wondered if she realized which word held the most emphasis. He knew.

Chapter 8

Jon lifted her into his arms. "Where?"

Tracy laid her head against his chest, loving the feeling of being carried. "My room. The next door on your right."

Jon kissed her once more before he walked out of the den. The hall was lit; her bedroom was not. The darkness closed around them, gentled by the light that spilled over from the hall. Jon laid her on the bed, lying down beside her after kicking off his shoes.

"We're still in our clothes," Tracy murmured softly, puzzled.

"I'm in no hurry. I want you to be comfortable, not rushed." He touched the ties that held her robe together, using the ends to feather the length of her throat until Tracy shivered in response. "Besides, there are all kinds of ways to give pleasure. Clothes can be a stimulant." He slid his hand down her throat, his fingers slipping lower to trace the curve of her breast through the fabrics.

Tracy arched, twisting in pleasure at the faintly rough rub of the cloth over her sensitive nipple. "Two can play at this game." She slipped her hands under his jacket, easing it from his shoulders. "But we have to start even." The sight of his holster and gun made her hesitate.

He stifled a curse as he felt her pause and realized the reason. "I should have remembered." He started to raise up to strip the weapon from his body.

Tracy stopped him. "Don't. Let me."

Their eyes met, his searching, hers determined.

Again she had proved herself to be unlike any woman he had known. Her eyes were clear, bright, passion merging with acceptance. "You're sure?"

"It's part of you. To deny the gun and the job you do would be to deny you. I can't do that and give my body to you. If you expect me to, then we should stop now. I gave myself to one man while not opening my eyes to what he was. I won't do that again."

"And I gave myself to a woman who said she could handle my profession and the fact that I wore a gun. She cried many times when I left for work. We both hated what she became but we tried to live with it." He didn't want to think about Amanda now, to remember the days when he had thought about leaving the force. But Tracy had a right to know at least a part of what drove him.

"We both got burned."

"In spades. I won't ask any woman for that again."

Tracy hadn't expected the hurt she'd feel, so she was unprepared to defend herself against it. Her eyes went dark with pain. Jon saw and understood. Tracy was a woman for commitment, and he was a man who wouldn't make one.

"Where do we go from here?" he asked.

Tracy looked in his eyes, seeing torment, need, yearning and the loneliness that she knew by heart. In that moment she made a decision she knew she might live to regret. "Right where we are. Neither of us sees roses and both of us need the beauty. Daisies can be pretty in their own way."

"You can be satisfied with that."

"I can try. So can you." Even as she said the words, some part of her knew she wanted more. Perhaps she wasn't as brave as she wished. She reached for his gun and this time he didn't try to stop her unbuckling it and taking it off.

"Maybe I was wrong. I don't think slow will do it, after all. Maybe next time." Jon untied the ribbons at her throat, lifting her with one arm to slide the robe from her body. The thin nightgown was close to transparent.

"Next time," she agreed huskily as she unfastened the buttons on his shirt.

The hair sprinkling his chest drew her eyes. Tangling her fingers in the mat she tugged gently. He responded with a bruising kiss that stole her breath and heated her blood. When he pulled her gown over her head she tossed his shirt on the floor.

Just looking at her watching him was destroying what little control he had left. He removed his slacks himself, and returned to her with more haste than grace. He had never felt so on fire for a woman in his life. His size and strength demanded he take care. "Talk to me. Give me a reason not to rush."

Tracy could see the effort he was making not to reduce their passion to an appeasement of need. "We have all night."

Jon inhaled deeply, feeling her trust diffuse the need to capture and hold. How she had the power to reach him was beyond his understanding. He only knew that it existed. "All night." He stroked her skin, finding pleasure and an easing of the claws of desire buried in his soul with the warmth and silken feel. Her moan of delight tasted good on his lips, the way she touched him in return even better. "More."

"Greedy man," she whispered, caressing lower. His hips fit hers as though they were meant to join with her alone.

He cupped her breasts, enjoying their lush curves. "Delicious," he said hoarsely. His head slowly lowered to one taut nipple. Wrapping his tongue around the peak he sucked gently and then with growing strength.

Tracy moaned, arching up to his mouth. Her arms slid around his neck and pulled him to her in a fierce possessiveness she was barely aware of. Jon's lips glided over her breasts to her stomach at the second his hand slipped into the dark curls below. She writhed in his arms at the dual claiming, vibrantly alive to every breath Jon took, every move he made. Tension filled her, demanding release.

"No, please," she pleaded, stroking his length, feeling the hardness grow in her hands. "I want you now."

Jon moved against her fingers, his eyes closed at the pleasure she gave so freely. When she guided him closer, demanding with a touch what her lips had spoken, he gave in to the passion screaming for release. With one smooth motion he joined them as one, feeling her wrap around him like a living velvet glove. He moved slowly at first, giving her a chance to catch his rhythm. When she responded with an eager thrust of her hips, he was lost.

Tracy took all he gave, wanting more. With every stroke, he gave her pleasure almost beyond bearing. His hands were hard on her shoulders but she was barely aware of it. Her whole being was centered in the fusing of his flesh to hers. Higher, harder, faster. The more he gave, the more she wanted. Her breath tore through her chest, her fingers gripped him tight. The tension built to the threshold of pain then splintered in a blinding rush of release. She cried aloud at the beauty, hearing his voice echo hers as they tumbled together to reality, their limbs together on dampened sheets.

Jon's breath was coming in small jerks, his heart beating wildly. "Woman, you are lethal," he whispered, his words stirring the tendrils of hair at her temple. "And beautiful and sexier than I can tell you."

"And you're dynamite. Not nice at all." She kissed his shoulders where her fingers had left their marks. "I hurt you."

Jon lifted his head. "Honey, if that's hurt let's do some more. You gave me more pleasure than I knew existed." He stroked the hair back from her face. "I could sleep for a week, and yet I don't want to miss a minute of holding you in my arms.''

"What about your work?"

"It's not going anywhere." He rolled on his back and settled her on his chest. "But I'll get up if that's what you want."

"Are you crazy? Do I look as if I want to move or want you to move?" Tracy knew they were playing games to cover the real meaning of their questions. He would not push for the right to sleep in her bed but he wanted it. And she wanted it, far more than she wanted to admit or wanted him to know.

"What time is your alarm set for?"

"Six."

"How do you feel about five?"

"Why?"

He grinned at the puzzled question. "I figure we'll both be rested by then. I wouldn't want to be late to work."

Tracy laughed softly, getting the picture. "Neither would I."

He pulled her closer, enjoying her laughter as he had few things in a long time. "Are you very sleepy?" His body was relaxed but not down for the count. He nudged her gently.

Tracy kissed his chest, her lips lightly tracing his nipple. His gasp of pleasure delighted her. "Not really. What do you have in mind?" She couldn't remember a time when she'd found so much joy in lovemaking. Nor could she remember wanting to reach for the peak again in so short a time. She had been satisfied, but he had only scratched the surface of her need. Curious, but not willing to delve too deeply when the moment held so much promise, she kissed him again.

Jon rolled her over to trap her beneath him. "Keep that up and we'll both find out what I have in mind."

Her eyes gleamed with challenge as her hands found him again. "Go for it," she whispered huskily.

Tracy woke slowly, conscious of Jon sleeping beside her. She smiled as she stretched. Tiny aches made her aware of her body in new ways. Her smile deepened. Three times. Each more beautiful than the last. Jon was a perfect lover, gentle and demanding by turns. He gave as freely as he took, liking her ability to arouse him, sometimes even demanding it. Until now that freedom had been a concept rather than a reality. She had been bound by the experiences she'd had with Lee. There was no sharing with him. She'd felt only a satisfaction of her physical need, despite his fervent and frequent avowals of love. Lee had initiated her into the sex act, but Jon had taught her how to make love.

"That smile would make a saint nervous," Jon said groggily, studying Tracy through half-closed eyes.

Tracy snuggled against him, laughing softly when she felt his body tighten with the touch of her hand. "I'm the one who should be nervous." He felt so good. Warm and strong. He had stayed close to her all night, his head more often than not pressed against her breast.

He lifted her onto his chest, fitting her intimately to him. "I usually don't like mornings, but I think with you they could become my favorite part of the day."

He took her lips in a lazy kiss. "Although the night wasn't bad, either," he added when he lifted his head.

"Rat," she accused a little breathlessly.

"Witch." He caressed her back as he nuzzled at her breast, his tongue finding one erect peak. "You were put on this earth to drive me mad." He nipped gently, easily controlling her body as she arched against him.

"I've never felt like this before," she confessed, wanting him to know the truth.

"Neither have I." The second breast received its kiss.

Tracy moaned, feeling the tension build. She had to touch him, give to him as he gave to her. Her hands flowed over his flesh, delighting in the male contours, learning new places that made him gasp and twist in her arms. His fingers stroked her body, bringing fire to sear her senses. Heat and desire. Potent combinations when Jon was the cause.

She didn't know where he began and she ended. Though they had yet to join, Tracy felt as though Jon were some wonderful part of herself that she had only just discovered. "Touch me," she demanded, the words rough with need and passion.

"I am," Jon whispered back, his fingers slipping between her thighs to the center of her heat. Soft, yielding, hot and tight. She was all that he had thought never to find in a woman and more. Her response was honest, deeper than the night had been long and more vibrant than the birth of a new day. "I can't wait any longer. Please."

Tracy laughed softly, her hands guiding him to her. "Can't you tell?" she breathed as she kissed him.

For one moment Jon poised above her, savoring her surrender even as he realized his own captivity. Then he joined them with one smooth, deep thrust. Her eyes gleamed with passion; her skin was slick with desire's dew. Her scent was rich, woman-ripe and compelling. His hands tightened on her body as he felt his arousal reach a new peak of pain pleasure. "It wasn't supposed to be like this," he said hoarsely as he gave in to the need to bury himself deep within her.

"I know," Tracy agreed huskily, arching against him.

His control broke as her hips clenched around him. Tracy watched his face with each stroke, finding his expression an erotic stimulus to his possession. Never had she participated so fully in making love, never had she wanted a man more. His groans were treasures as she reached higher and higher, binding him to her as they thrust for the fulfillment they both craved. The fire grew brighter, their bodies grew taut with need. Flesh to flesh with only the moisture from the heat they generated to separate them, they moved together. For one brief moment, the union was complete. For one instant, they danced to the ancient rhythm as one. The climax was heralded by twin shouts of delight. Then it was done, the union over in a rush of release so sweet that neither had any defense against the gentle pleasure that followed the storm. Whether either had meant it or not, a tie had been made that would never be broken. The knowledge was in their eyes as they stared at each other in silence, both knowing words were no longer useful.

* * *

Tracy stared at the frying pan in her hand. She had to pull herself together. One stupid little scene, and she was so off balance she was trembling. Jon had looked so natural standing in her bedroom, pulling on his clothes while talking to her about their upcoming day. His smile had been intimate, a lover's look that told of pleasure and possession. She had worn that same smile until she felt the emotion slip into her heart. The smile had faded as the fear and wariness that had become so much a part of her took over.

Jon hadn't noticed how quickly she had beaten a retreat from the room. They had been running late and he had accepted her excuse of wanting to get breakfast started. Now she was facing herself and counting all the ways she had been a fool. Chemistry was not a good basis for emotion. She, more than most, knew that. Jon had given every indication he wanted no more from her than mutually shared passion. He was gentle, caring but so careful about keeping a part of himself aloof.

The sound of his footsteps in the hall made her pull herself together. She couldn't let him see her confusion. It wasn't his fault that she had made a mistake.

"How do you like your eggs?" Tracy set the skillet on the burner before going to the refrigerator for a carton of eggs. She held on to a desperate kind of friendliness, hoping he wouldn't notice anything unusual in her attitude. She didn't understand herself and until she did she would take no more risks.

Jon watched Tracy move about the kitchen, reading her discomfort. She looked no more at ease than he felt. He had tried to play the game, but Tracy simply didn't fit in the mold. He had watched her retreat from the bedroom and cursed himself for not being able to talk to her. It had been so easy the night before, but now neither of them knew what to do, how to act. Their need for each other had been too deep and too immediate. He needed space and time and suspected she did as well. But because of their situation, neither respite would be granted them. Sighing, he tried to think of a way to make things easier.

"You don't need to cook for me. I can get something on the way to the station." He couldn't walk away from her completely, but he could give her an hour or two without his presence. The extra-duty people the chief was arranging for her safety would be on the job by now.

"That's all right. I don't mind cooking for you." Tracy glanced at him. She tried to smile. "I'm not very good at this, I'm afraid."

Jon could see the tension in her body and the myriad emotions in her eyes. Suddenly, he couldn't allow her to feel embarrassed or uncomfortable with their passion. He didn't care that he was knowingly giving up the cushion of distance from emotional involvement. He knew only that he wanted to see a real smile on Tracy's face. "Neither am I. I didn't expect things to get so out of hand," he admitted honestly, closing the space between them. "You pack quite a punch, lovely lady, and I wasn't prepared. But I don't regret being with you, no matter what the future holds. I hope you don't regret it, either." Jon put his arms around her, prepared to let her go at the first sign of resistance.

Tracy looked into his eyes and saw the confusion and doubts she felt mirrored there. With a small sigh, she relaxed. He had been strong enough to confess his feelings, she could be no less. "I don't regret making love with you but I don't know what comes next. I need to know."

"I don't know, either, and I think I need to know, too," Jon said, watching her closely.

Tracy touched his cheek, the gesture feeling so natural she couldn't deny it. Maybe she hadn't been a fool. A man brave enough to voice his doubts and offer honesty was rare. "It's so risky. We don't want the same things."

"I know. But I can't walk away from you. Don't ask me to." He was crazy. His plan for never letting another woman mean everything to him was in danger of slipping into oblivion. He didn't care.

"I can't walk away from you, either."

"Then let things ride until this case is over. Maybe we're both letting circumstances create reality out of illusions."

Fear rippled over her at the truth neither could deny. "I'm scared."

"Don't be." He pulled her close, his lips brushing hers. "I'm here with you. We'll share whatever comes, and I'll do my best to protect you from the firebug."

Tracy felt his caring wrap around her like a warm blanket on a cold day. She hadn't expected the feeling and was all the more affected because of its appearance. "Who'll protect you?"

He smiled although it didn't reach his watchful eyes. "Are you volunteering for the job?"

She smiled back, seeing his surprise but not worried by it. She leaned into his strength, remembering the moments when he had been completely at her mercy. "I believe I am," she murmured, her voice holding a note of wonder that even she could hear.

His eyes softened with tenderness, an emotion he had thought burned out of him long ago. "Then I accept your offer." This time his kiss held passion, tenderness and a new feeling that left them both breathless. "Now, sit yourself down here and let me tell you about how I'm going to keep you safe from your watcher." He took a chair and pulled her into his lap.

She laughed softly. "You've got a lot of faith in my powers of concentration, my friend," she teased.

"That's not the only thing I'm beginning to think I have a lot of faith in," he returned cryptically. Before Tracy could comment on his remark, he launched into a description of the precautions being taken for her safety.

They ate a leisurely breakfast with none of the tension that had characterized the beginning of the morning. While Tracy cleaned up the kitchen, Jon walked around the yard, checking for further signs of the prowler before he took Tracy to work in his car.

Bo watched from the shadows. They were together. The cop had spent the night. He hadn't thought her that kind of woman. Where was her pride? The cop didn't want marriage. He was only taking advantage of a good thing while he tried to do his job. Bo frowned, hating the thought of her lying in that man's arms. She was meant for better. Or was she? Maybe she bedded with him because they were two of a kind. Maybe she wouldn't understand why he had set those fires. Maybe her soft voice was all an act. Lies. He hated them. Lies hurt. Lies killed the innocent. He had to know the truth about Tracy.

"You wanted to see me?" Jasper rose at Jon's entrance and held out his hand.

"We've got trouble." Jon didn't believe in sugar-coating the truth.

Jasper's eyes narrowed as he gestured Jon to a chair. "Explain."

"Since Tracy got involved with this arson thing she's been feeling as if she's being watched. She tried putting her reactions down to nervousness. It didn't work. Last night she called me at home with a prowler scare. I went over. It was too dark to see anything much, but I did check it out this morning. There's a slight chance that her prowler might not be related to this case, but I wouldn't bet my pension on it."

Jasper frowned deeply, saying nothing for a moment. "So what's the plan?"

Jon heaved a silent sigh of relief. The worst was over. He hadn't been sure that Jasper would listen. "I've arranged for Tracy's house to be watched by the local police. Until we can prove differently, we're going to work on the assumption that Bo is our arsonist. So far the guy has shown an amazing capacity to get away time and again. He's shown the police to be incapable of catching him. His luck has probably fostered a kind of 'I can do anything' belief in himself. I've seen it happen before. That kind of behavior can either be a help—he might just get cocky enough to make mistakes—or it might mean he quits worrying about hurting someone—assuming he's purposefully avoided causing any injuries—and gets careless."

"I don't want Tracy or any of my people hurt. You do what you have to make that a fact and I'll not fight you on anything you need. Ratings aren't as important as one life."

Jon nodded, glad of his attitude. "When I called in to the police station this morning I got word that we now have possible links with some fires in Georgia similar to ours. Because of that, we've started querying other nearby states, but we don't have any information back as yet."

Jasper sat forward in his chair, his curiosity on full alert. "Same pattern?"

"If you mean that there's *no* pattern to the buildings hit, then the answer is yes. Also no clues as to motive or the man's identity."

"I'll be damned."

"You have to remember that arson, especially when no loss of life is involved, is not as high a priority on our overworked schedules as crimes involving human injury. Every one of the cases we've investigated so far has been handled before as an isolated incident. We're the ones tying the ends together to make a whole. The picture is emerging slowly because of a lot of original guesswork that's turning out to be fact. If our mayor hadn't been one of the owners of the first building hit in this town, I'm not sure whether this would have fallen into our hands at all. That's off the record, of course."

Jasper grinned, liking the man sitting so relaxed in front of him. "I never would have thought otherwise. You aren't the kind to kiss and tell."

He shrugged off the compliment. "Not wise in my line of work." Jon got to his feet.

Jasper walked him to the door. "If you need anything from us, let me know."

"Now that you mention it, I need to become a bit of a fixture around here. Will that be a problem?"

Jasper looked at him, reading more than an easily filled request. "I thought there might be a plan somewhere in this," he murmured dryly. "No. You do what you have to do to protect Tracy. Become her shadow. You won't hear any complaints from this end."

"I thought you'd understand." Jon returned his dry look with interest.

"Better than you think. She's in the room at the end of the hall. You've got ten minutes until airtime, so I guess I'll be seeing you around for a while. Do you want me to take you to her?"

"I think I can find the way."

Chapter 9

Jon paused in the doorway of the radio station's staff room. He made use of the small alcove between the doorjamb and the edge of a fireplace to keep out of the way of those passing. The room was wall-to-wall desks, cluttered but with a definite air of organization. He was in no hurry to approach Tracy, preferring to watch for a moment unobserved. Tracy sat at one end of the room, her back to him, a phone tucked against her ear. She was making notes on the huge calendar blotter in front of her. Her voice was easy to listen to despite the sharpness of her questions. He was impressed with her ability to handle the caller. She'd just had a paper thrust in front of her for approval, and she still kept track of the phone conversation.

For the next five minutes he saw Tracy attempt to run to ground a very elusive politician, tracking him from his home to Washington, D.C. Although she failed to make connections she never lost patience or betrayed frustration, her manner with the last caller as gracious as with the first.

"Five minutes, Tracy." Nikki stopped at Tracy's desk and deposited a stack of news clippings on the blotter. "Lately, it seems as if everything breaks on the same day. A Middle East incident, this damn arsonist thing that keeps hanging around like a toothache and that blasted school board controversy."

Tracy laughed, grabbing up the stack of articles. "Thanks for setting these up for me. I didn't have time to cut them out myself. I wonder if anyone realizes what we do to keep up with the news?"

"I feel like a coupon clipper every morning of my life. I swear I have dreams with little highlighted articles running after me yelling, 'Take me, take me. I'm the most important.'"

Jon shifted away from his resting place, drawn toward Tracy. Her laughter was music to beguile. He moved toward the sound, wanting a share of her warmth. A smile tilted his lips as he enjoyed the picture Nikki had drawn of her nightmare. He didn't fully understand the reference but it didn't matter.

"Do they catch you?" he asked.

Tracy turned in her chair, her eyes wide with surprise. "I didn't realize you were still here. Surely Jasper didn't keep you this long."

"No, I just thought I'd continue my education on how a radio station works." He glanced at Nikki, relieved that Tracy no longer looked at him with wariness in her beautiful eyes. "Do you really have dreams about demanding articles?"

"We go through a stack of papers and magazines every day, looking for articles that might tempt our audience's palate. Every one of us has a particular style, certain things that pique our interest. We cut out what draws our eye and mount them on paper for reference. Sometimes a caller phones and quotes one of these little gems, or we use the articles as jump-off points for a show."

Tracy rose and collected her material. "Much as I'd like to stay and chat, I have a show to do." Just for an instant she acknowledged that she really did want to stay and talk to Jon. She was beginning to realize what having made love with Jon had done to her. She could no longer keep her distance, pretending that her emotions weren't touched. Annoyed with her weakness after only one night spent in Jon's arms, she added, "If there's anything you need, Jon, I'm sure Nikki would be more than glad to help you." She only managed a step away before Jon's hand on her arm halted her progress. Looking over her shoulder, she encountered a knowing, almost sympathetic smile.

"I'm sure she would be a great help, but Jasper gave me to you. Besides, I thought we had gotten past either of us running this morning," he added in a voice only she could hear.

Tracy shivered at the strength in his response and the way she needed to be reminded that she had agreed to take the risk of letting him close. She sighed, disgusted with her hot-and-cold behavior. "You're right, we did." She eased her arm from his grasp with a faint grimace. "I'm just not used to it yet," she added with a quick look at the clock. "I have to go or I'll be late."

Jon followed her, enjoying the sway of her trim hips beneath her slim gray skirt. The scarlet blouse in a silky fabric kept the outfit from becoming drab and ordinary. She looked sleek, completely professional and utterly feminine, and he had the insane desire to touch his lips to the nape of her neck and feel her quiver in his arms. The memory of their passion clouded his mind, driving out the thoughts of the job. For one moment he wished he had exclusive right to Tracy's time and thoughts.

The idea brought him up short, a cold splash of reality to douse the flame of desire. He traveled best alone and unfettered, he reminded himself. Although he could make his way in another world, this one was his choice. He was no nine-to-five man, and he had learned the folly of visions of a woman in his home on a permanent basis, kiddies in the upstairs rooms and a dog in the yard. Tracy was a lovely, passionate woman, but he was a fool to think of ties. She had given him no indication that she wanted more than they were sharing, and he was glad. With that thought in mind, he spoke quickly and concisely, explaining in greater detail the protection she'd get until Bo was caught.

Tracy stopped short, her eyes wide with surprise and dismay. "You can't be serious? I know you said this morning that I would be watched, but I didn't realize you meant as closely as this." She shook her head. "You've got a job to do. You can't possible have time to start dogging my footsteps."

Jon controlled his impatience. "This guy could be dangerous. Torches do not generally follow people home. You live alone and I don't want you to become a statistic. On top of that, we need you safe so that you can help us get this guy. So far you are our strongest link.''

"And Jasper agreed to this?"

"He can see the need." Jon watched her, knowing he could force the issue but not wanting to.

Tracy stared into his eyes, seeing the rock-hard determination for her to agree. His reasons were logical and necessary. She was neither a fool nor the material of which heroes were made. Last night's prowler had scared her. But neither could she tolerate being thrown into Jon's exclusive company for who knew how long. She was already laboring under the changes he had brought to her life. Her emotions were out of control, her choices dictated by feelings she didn't want to acknowledge, much less give in to.

"I know this isn't what you want—"

Tracy interrupted him before he could finish. "All right. You've made your point." She tried a faint smile, wondering if it looked as stiff as it felt. "I'm just not accustomed to being without a certain amount of privacy."

"Tracy, what are you doing out here? It's airtime." Walter poked his head into the corridor, frowning heavily.

"I'm on my way." Tracy slipped by Jon, trying to put Bo, Jon and the case out of her mind. She had a show to do that would take all her concentration. She'd handle the rest later. "You'll have to stay in here." Tracy stopped, gesturing to the chair beside a massive control board. "You've already met Walter, our director."

Jon barely acknowledged the pleasant-faced man who nodded without taking his hands and eyes from the myriad knobs and dials before him. "Why can't I sit in there with you?"

Tracy could think of two reasons but offered only one, the least important. "The mikes are very sensitive. They pick up the smallest sound. It's hard to remember to be careful for two solid hours." She smiled a little to take any possible sting from her refusal. She pushed open the door connecting the two rooms as the news report that separated her program from the one before was ending.

Jon took his chair, feeling a little cramped in the close quarters. The equipment had plenty of space, leaving the humans to adapt their positions to the small area remaining.

"Looks like I've been landed in your lap again," he murmured as Nikki squeezed in beside him to a place in front of a small computer terminal and keyboard. A multibutton phone console hung on the wall above the monitor.

"I never mind having a sexy man sitting in my lap," Nikki teased with a smile.

Through the large window between the rooms, Jon watched Tracy get ready for her show. She was less than four feet away but he couldn't reach her or touch her. It was a strange yet familiar feeling. He shifted, not liking the direction of his thoughts. He had never before had trouble concentrating on his job. Granted, the need to make himself more visible in Tracy's life had both professional and personal merit, but it should not give way to this need to possess. To share was one thing. To be caught and vulnerable was another.

"Will it ruin your concentration if I ask questions?"

"Be my guest. There's no telling how busy we'll be with calls. Tracy's discussing the town budget hearing that's coming up next week. Last night the mayor had some very pithy comments to make at a dinner party. The papers were full of it this morning."

Tracy slipped on the earphones, feeling too aware of Jon on the other side of the glass. Why did she have to be touched by a man who had made it clear from the beginning that he was in her life temporarily? Good sense should have directed that she keep some sort of emotional distance between them. But good sense was on a holiday. Having held him in her arms, known the intimate possession and gentleness of his body mated with hers, she had lost her objectivity. Jon mattered. Too much. She couldn't remember a time in her life when she had let a man interfere in her work.

She wanted to deny the feeling of pleasure that finding him standing in front of her desk had spawned. She wanted to deny the fact that he made her as nervous as a cat with a long tail in a room full of rocking chairs. She wanted to deny the memory of the time spent in his arms and the way she had given to him so freely. But wanting and being able to do something were two different things. Honesty was a point of honor with her, whether it was her own or someone else's. Jon bothered her. She suspected she bothered him in more than just physical ways. Once she had caught a look in his eye that hinted at internal anger at his own susceptibility. She had recognized the look because she felt the same way, and she'd stored it in her mind. A strange thing for her to know and accept in her lover or herself, but yet again, though she wanted to deny it, she could not.

Walter cued her, though he didn't have to. She responded, trying to blot out Jon's presence with the needs of her show.

"She's really good," Jon murmured. Almost two hours had passed, each minute bringing a deeper understanding of Tracy and the medium she clearly loved. "I don't think I'll ever be able to listen to the radio again without appreciating the work going on behind the scenes. I had no idea where commercials came from, never even thought about it." He glanced over his shoulder to the solid wall of eight-track tape racks that stretched from floor to ceiling. "News bulletins coming down from the network. Wall Street reports. I thought I was fairly observant but I sure missed this stuff before."

Nikki grinned before fielding another caller. The lines had been buzzing with determined regularity. The budget issue was proving to be a hotly contested battle, with Tracy playing today's referee. The monitor in front of her showed all but one of the five phone lines filled. Nikki punched in the information then sat back with a sigh.

"You make me tired just watching you."

"At least we're almost done with this one. We'll be lucky if we get through more than this call and one more."

He chuckled at her tart answer. "Do I hear a silent 'thank heaven' in that remark?"

"You bet your sweet life," she agreed fervently.

Jon glanced at Tracy, wondering how she kept her cool at the fast pace. She still looked and sounded as though she were easing through a nice day. Her calls had ranged from polite to downright nasty. The woman who had shivered from fear of a prowler the night before was nowhere in evidence today. A moment later he revised his opinion.

"Damn that man!" he swore, watching Tracy's face go still, paling slightly as the sound of Bo's voice filled the control room. He barely heard Nikki's disgusted exclamation over her failure to recognize Bo.

"Hi, Tracy, remember me? It's Bo."

Tracy's hand clenched on the paper she held. This time she would not be afraid. She was tired of this guy hounding her. She laid the sheet down carefully, striving to keep her tone level, unaffected. "I understand you have some comments on the budget issue," she said, looking directly at Jon.

"No, the woman who answered the phone assumed I did. You and I have some unfinished business."

"What kind of business?" Jon looked ready to leap down the phone line and snatch Bo through the receiver by his hair. The image eased her temper, allowing her to relax slightly.

"I want to get back to the firebug. He knows you and he's watching you. He has a job to do, but he wants you to know he won't hurt anyone to do it."

The intimacy of his comments was like mud clinging to her skin. Tracy wanted to rub her arms to escape the feel. "What kind of a job?" she asked carefully, knowing that Jon needed her to keep Bo talking in the hopes the man would drop a clue a two.

"He's not just setting fires for fun."

"You sound as if you know him," she murmured, holding her breath in the hope Bo would acknowledge that he was the firebug.

"I do." Bo heard her interest and responded to it. Relaxing for the first time since he had seen that cop car in her drive, he added, "Very well." Despite the fact she slept with the cop, she was still willing to listen, to understand.

"Tell me about him," Tracy invited, glancing at the clock and silently cursing the minutes ticking away. The show was almost over.

Bo laughed, delighted that Tracy wanted to know more. No one had cared when it was important to him, but now that the shoe was on the other foot he had the eyes and ears of Tracy and her audience.

"I'll tell you anything you want to know soon. But not today. I will give you one clue. The firebug has a very good reason for every one of his fires." He sobered, remembering that reason. "Find that reason and you have the key." He hung up the phone, smiling at his own cleverness. They wouldn't find the key but they would keep trying. Like ants at a picnic they would wrestle a huge crumb when any number of small ones, more easily taken, went by the wayside.

Jon rose the moment it was clear the caller had hung up. Sensitive mike or not he wouldn't sit there a moment longer without touching Tracy. She was signing off for the day as he opened the studio's door. He hardly heard her theme music as he closed the distance between them, remembering just in time not to take her in his arms and give the gossips something to cut their teeth on.

"Are you all right?"

She tried a smile, hoping it looked more natural than it felt. "Not completely but I'll make it."

"He's calling every day now."

She nodded although he had not made his comment a question. "He's becoming more familiar. I hate that." She crossed her arms, feeling cold. "I swear I would recognize his voice among a hundred others, with or without the disguise. It's in the way he says his words. Some radio people have that kind of ability." She picked up her papers and started out of the room, needing a little of what could be called privacy in the cramped station. Jon stayed at her side although it was a tight fit in some places. They didn't speak until she sat down at her desk and he took a chair beside her.

"I think I'm glad I have you watching over me now that I think about it. Sorry for the argument earlier." She lifted her eyes to his.

Jon inhaled sharply at her fear and determination to see the situation through to its conclusion. He wanted to hold her, blot out the future that neither of them might be able to control. He settled for touching her hand, his fingers lingering on the soft skin, because he couldn't risk taking her in his arms. "I won't let anything happen to you," he promised.

Tracy stared at him, feeling the warmth of his touch and strength of his vow to keep her safe. Her last defense crumbled in the dust. Trust, pure as the first snow in the mountains, flickered to life. She smiled shakily before returning the pressure of his hand on hers. "I know."

In that one look she had given what no other person, including Amanda, had ever offered. Jon felt the gift settle in his heart, weakening his resolve still further. Without anything but her own belief to go on Tracy had handed him her trust. In that moment, he wished with all his heart he were a man made for commitment.

Bo stared at the phone, wishing he had told her the truth. Only the thought of their audience had kept him silent. He glanced at the phone book on the table in front of him. He wanted to talk to her again when he didn't have to worry who was listening. He knew her address and her name. Was she listed? Pulling the book toward him, he slowly turned the pages. She wasn't in the book but there was still a chance that she was simply out of the directory. Lots of single women were. He dialed information and then hung up, smiling. He had her number! An omen. He believed in them. He had to rush or he would be late for work. But tonight, when he was alone in the building, he would call her. Tonight he would tell her who he was.

"How did it go? I listened to the show. That guy gives me the creeps," Roger said as Jon took his place at the desk facing his.

"Not bad." Roger was fishing, and Jon wasn't in the mood to make it easy for him. They had been together too long for his partner not to realize that Tracy was becoming more important in his life with each day.

"That was a long lunch. It's after two."

Jon leaned back in his chair and gave Roger a straight look. "Since when did you become a clock watcher?"

"Since I got this." Roger tossed a stapled sheaf of papers onto Jon's blotter. "Cast your eyes over that little ditty."

The only time Roger showed any emotion other than cynicism was when he had snagged a lead. Jon's brows rose at the eager anticipation that was visible now. He looked down, then looked closer on seeing the computer readout of a list of fires from West Palm Beach to a small town in Virginia. He swore softly as he read the total. Thirty-seven.

"No one has linked them together before?"

"Crazy, isn't it? There isn't an office between here and Virginia that isn't steaming. Every one of them had practically the same thing to say. No loss of life, no definite pattern to the hits, and every fire had enough of a different method to create questions concerning the torch being the same man. And more important, the fires seemed to start without reason and stop the same way." Roger propped his elbows on his desk, watching Jon's mind go into high gear. "With insurance reimbursing the owners for the losses, and no deaths or injuries, most of these cases just got filed when the firebug blew out of town."

"The guy must have some sort of list. It's the only thing that makes sense. Random hits when he goes to so much trouble to plan this out just don't compute."

"Agreed."

"If he has a list then he has a motive, which definitely ties in with what our firebug said to Tracy this morning."

"The chief was spitting and sputtering around here, going on about the nerve of the guy and how he'd have his rump in a sling as soon as possible."

Jon's eyes flickered with amusement, before going abruptly serious. "Tracy's from Virginia," he said, stating the fact they both knew from Tracy's background check.

"The connection could be that this Bo character recognizes her voice, maybe he was even a fan back home."

"He's probably disguising his voice to hide an accent. This would also explain the familiarity with his speech that's been driving Tracy nuts."

"It's possible."

"I wonder if the sound director has any tricks to clean up the distortion."

"Now that's a good idea. You give him a call while I see if I can't put a rush on the employment records of this last group of companies. I want to be sure the lists we were given are complete."

"This is one time when I'm glad we have computers. Cross-checking those records by hand for duplicate personnel would take days."

Roger laughed as he got to his feet. "And drive me crazy."

Jon picked up the phone and called the radio station, then waited for Walter to come on the line. A minute later he hung up. Although he was annoyed with himself for not having thought of this angle sooner, he was satisfied with the answers he had received. It was possible to doctor the station's tape of the shows so that Bo's calls could be isolated and brought more sharply into focus. The success of removing the distortion depended on a number of factors, but Walter had promised to do his best and get back to Jon with the results as soon as possible.

Having done all he could for the moment, Jon decided to take another ride out to Tracy's house. He had only been able to take a quick look around this morning. Now he wanted to take his time. Maybe their prowler had gotten careless and left a footprint, a burned-out match, a stub of a cigarette, something.

It was late afternoon when he returned to the office with nothing to show for his time but a better appreciation of the task Tracy had set herself when she had bought her house. The property was in an excellent location, the view beautiful and the yard and exterior of the house a mess. She needed a helper and he was going to be that man. Until this situation was over he would be sticking to her side like a polyester blouse in midsummer.

Chapter 10

"An end to another day." Nikki stopped at Tracy's desk and leaned her hip against its edge. "Remind me never to buy new shoes and then wear them to work without breaking them in first. Am I ever glad I don't have to go home and cook for a husband and kids tonight. I can soak my tired, aching feet, curl up with a good book and be lazy."

Tracy finished the file she had been working on and slipped it into the top drawer. "I told you those high heels would kill you."

"But they were exactly the right color for that new suit I bought. You know I can't resist sexy shoes."

Tracy laughed. "Being gorgeous tends to have a price tag." She collected her handbag and briefcase.

The two women walked to the rear door, exchanging remarks with those they passed. The heat was an oppressive blanket as they stepped outside. Both paused.

"Looks like you're going to have a more interesting night than I am."

Tracy followed Nikki's look to see Jon leaning against the side of his car, which was parked in the slot next to hers.

"You didn't tell me you had a date," Nikki continued.

"I don't tell you everything. I need some secrets," she murmured teasingly. She moved toward Jon. With every step she felt lighter, less tired and more glad to see him. His smile found a reflection on her lips. "Have I kept you waiting long?"

"No." Jon pushed away from his car to open the passenger door. Tracy slipped in, waving to Nikki as her friend got into her own car.

Tracy watched Jon walk around to get into the driver's seat. Suddenly she had an almost overwhelming urge to lean her head on his shoulder and let him take the weight of what was happening away from her. Her fears about the firebug made her feel bad enough, but their growing relationship made her even more nervous. She wanted to tell Jon about Lee and talk to him about her past. She wanted more than his professional support and his presence in her bed. She wanted . . . love. The word came out of nowhere, momentarily taking her breath away. She hadn't expected it, had missed all the clues that it was happening. In short, she had walked right in like a lamb to the slaughter with a man who gave every indication he didn't believe in forever.

Jon felt the tension invade her body and saw the sudden pallor to her skin. Concerned, he took her arm, half-afraid she was going to faint. "Are you all right?" he demanded.

Tracy shook off the weakness, grabbed hold of her nerve and dug deep for courage. She loved this man and she wanted him to love her back. Those two facts stood out in her mind as though printed on a billboard. She couldn't order love, but she certainly could nurture what they shared.

"I'm tired and hungry." She made herself pull away.

Jon let her go, positive for the first time in their relationship that she was lying to him. He watched her for a moment, wanting to demand answers and knowing he didn't have the right. "Both things are easily fixed," he murmured finally before starting the car. "Why don't you lean back and relax. Doze if you want until we get home."

Both noticed the word *home*, but neither commented on it.

Bo watched Tracy and Kent, his fists balled at his sides. He hadn't wanted to believe that Tracy would continue to consort with the man the newspapers had said was assigned to catch him. The cop's picture had been included in the article as though the man was a celebrity or something. He had hated that, just as he hated watching Kent and Tracy grow closer. Now he was even picking her up from work and taking her home . . . to bed. Kent was becoming her shadow. He couldn't allow that. He turned away, stalking to his car and getting in. He had to find a way to come between them. He needed Tracy but Kent was a risk to his plan. He looked at the phone number on the paper tucked into his sun visor. It was time to make contact with Tracy outside the station lines although the risk was greater here. He knew and accepted that, but he needed her.

Jon followed Tracy into her house, watching her carefully. She was still pale and seemed so brittle she looked as if she would shatter if he touched her. He went to her, taking her in his arms, needing to hold her. "What is it, honey? Is this case tearing you up this badly?"

Tracy searched his eyes, seeing in them concern and a little tenderness but none of the love that filled her being. "I need to talk about us and where we're going and where we've been." It was a toss-up who was more startled by the blunt demand.

Jon lifted his head. "Why now? Things were all right this morning. Or at least I thought they were."

Tracy pulled away, sighing. Wrapping her arms around her middle, she studied him. "I don't know, Jon. This whole situation seems so unreal to me. I keep telling myself that I understand. You touch me and I go up in smoke. We come so near to being close and then one of us pulls away. I hurt and I don't know why. I need to know why."

Jon paced the room, understanding her desire because it echoed his own. He glanced at her, seeing the agony of confusion in her expression. "Soul-baring time?"

"Don't you think we deserve it? Or is chemistry without substance all we have?"

He came to her then, unable to bear the thought himself or to allow her to think such a thing of either of them. "No, it isn't just chemistry." He caught her arms, pulling her close. "But it could be this unreal situation."

"No!" She lifted her eyes to his, glaring at him. "Don't give me that. I won't believe it. You have too much experience and I have too many reasons why I wouldn't be fooled this way."

Their eyes met, neither of them certain, both wanting to be. Jon sighed deeply before releasing her to move toward the couch. "All right. My history then yours. Fair trade?"

Tracy stared at him as he sat down, stretching his legs out before him in a relaxed position that didn't go with the intense expression on his face. Without thinking she took a seat at the other end of the couch, close enough to touch but not touching him. "I'm listening." The bleakness of his eyes almost made her regret her need to know. Without a word being spoken, she knew what she was asking of him had a terrible price.

"I had a woman in my life. She said she could handle my work. I was a year out of college and fell into a drug situation that sent me undercover, deep undercover. I was in for eleven months. Eleven long months of playing at being a criminal, of not seeing Amanda because it was too dangerous for both of us, of not knowing what she was doing, of not being able to take enough showers to wash off the stench of the life I was leading."

Jon's words were harsh as he drew forth ugliness from the dark corners of his mind.

"Finally, we solved the case. I came out to the world I had left behind, but nothing was the same. I functioned, I made love with Amanda—she had waited for me—I worked my shift and took the congratulations of my friends. Amanda was pregnant by the time the case came to trial. The D.A. should have had an airtight case, but he didn't. We walked into that courtroom expecting to send this guy up for life on counts ranging from murder to dope peddling, and he got off." Jon's hands clenched into fists at his sides, rage apparent in his tone.

Tracy raised her head, to stare into his eyes. Right now he didn't see her. He saw only the past. She waited, somehow knowing the worst was to come.

"The guy made threats against all three of us who'd been involved in nailing him. The department did the best they could at protecting us and our families. I pleaded with Amanda to leave town until the thing was settled, but she refused. One of the men was killed in a traffic accident. Another had his house burned to the ground. Luckily he and his family had decided on the spur of the moment to take off for a weekend at the Keys without telling anyone. The fire department said that if they had been in the house they wouldn't have survived. He had four children."

"My God," Tracy whispered. "What happened to you and Amanda?"

"Before I had gone undercover, Amanda had fought the battle that anyone who cares about a law-enforcement person fights. She faced my work and the danger that it represents. At first she handled it well, but even before I went undercover I could tell she was beginning to feel the strain. It wasn't in anything that she said. It was more a look in her eyes when I strapped on my gun. She stuck it out when I came back but sometimes I'd catch her with tears in her eyes. Still, we were happy when we found out she was pregnant. We both welcomed the thought of a baby. We were naive, but we thought if she had someone to love and care for besides me, maybe she could cope better." He inhaled deeply, bracing himself for the last. He could delay no longer.

"As I said, she wouldn't leave. I wanted her to but she refused. Maybe it was her pride that demanded she stick it out with me. I don't know. But she stayed. Toward the last we had a policewoman with her when I wasn't. The department got a line on the guy again. I was the bait but Amanda didn't know. The scenario went down just as we planned. The threat was gone. I can remember how free I felt as I went home that day. I walked in. The policewoman was there but Amanda wasn't. She'd heard that we caught the guy, so she'd taken the car out to buy champagne to celebrate. A drunk plowed into her car about a mile from home. Neither of them survived. I lost her and my child."

Tracy felt the tears slide down her face but she didn't try to stop them. Amanda and Jon deserved her grief.

For Jon the rest was less difficult to describe. "I raged for days afterward. I knew as well as anyone that the situation was an unusual one and that Amanda's accident was just that. But I learned something else, too. Even if Amanda had lived, our relationship wouldn't have survived. It wasn't because we didn't love or try to make it work. My profession is hell on marriages and relationships. I don't know one family

that hasn't had major trouble in facing and winning
the battle of sending the cop out the door with his gun
strapped on. We get precious little respect from the
people we are sworn to protect and serve, our children are targets for every bully, our spouses band to
together to handle the stress because civilians can't
understand even if they want to. I won't put anyone I
care about through that kind of torture."

He looked down at her then, seeing her tears. He
lifted his thumbs to brush the silver streaks dry. "I
never meant to hurt you. I should have walked away
but I can't. Yes, this case holds me here, but not as
you do. The feel of you and your smile reach into me
and make me wish things were different."

Tracy stared into his eyes and read his pain and his
need for her there. His past was so much cleaner than
her own. She didn't want him to know of the mistake
she had made, but she couldn't refuse to finish what
she had started. "It's my turn now." She wrapped her
fingers around his wrists and drew his hands from her
face. "I wish I had never started this but I want to
finish. I want you to know why I needed to know
about you and, in knowing, made you hurt." She
smiled sadly. "You had a lovely woman and a baby.
Right or wrong, you and Amanda were trying to build
something solid. I had lies from a married man. I gave
three years of my life to Lee, believing we were making a future. I believed in him, missed him when he
was on the road traveling and planned my life to steal
precious moments with him when he was home. I
loved him, I thought, and he said he loved me.

"Then one morning I discovered a man will lie to
take a woman, to hold her, to own her. About an hour

after I kissed Lee goodbye for his long run to the Atlanta office for a monthly field report, there was a knock at my door. Stupid me, I thought Lee had forgotten something. I raced to answer it. It wasn't Lee. It was a very pregnant little mouse of a woman with tears in her eyes. I'll give you one guess who she was married to.'' She met Jon's eyes, her memories painfully clear.

"I held her hand while she begged me not to take her husband, not to leave her two other children without their father. You lost your dream for a future to an accident. I lost nothing more than an illusion. I came here to build a new, clean life. I want a home and a family so I made this place, but I made no room in my heart for a man. Until you. I didn't want to care but I do. But I don't trust what I'm feeling and that frightens me.''

Jon took her in his arms, ignoring her resistance. He couldn't bear the pain he saw in her eyes. "Let me hold you, honey," he whispered, tucking her close to his heart. Laying his cheek on her dark hair, he searched for the words to ease her guilt and hurt. "It wasn't your fault. Not all liars are detectable. You went into the relationship for all the best reasons and he cheated. As for being frightened, you don't have the corner on that market. I didn't want to care either but I do, and now I don't know what to do about you.''

Tracy held onto him, finding comfort in his embrace and the words he poured over her wounded soul. "Two lame birds," she mumbled. "Neither of us believe in forever.''

"But *you* should. You belong with a man who can give you a beautiful life. I can't do that. My work isn't clean and neither am I anymore. Roger calls us the city's garbage detail. He's right. I can work at something else. In fact I could not work at all and still live well. I now own a half interest in three very successful restaurants. But I won't quit. Someone has to fight the battle and I'm good at what I do. I made the choice but I'll never ask another woman to share it with me."

Tracy made herself listen, but she heard more than his words. She saw his soul, which carried scars to match her own. There were no words that would put the past right for either of them. There was only the present. Tracy tightened her hold, wanting to take his pain as her own.

Jon allowed himself one more moment to hold her then he lifted her away from him. He held her eyes as he said, "My life hasn't changed, yours has. You're wasting yourself trying to be less than you could be. Look at this place. It shows the woman you really are. You want a home and children. You won't find that with me."

She lifted her chin, her sympathy and understanding turning to something approaching anger. "I don't recall asking you to provide me with either."

Jon's temper slipped from his control. He didn't want Tracy to settle for what little he could give her. She deserved more. The idea of her spending a second—much less a lifetime—with another man was like acid in his soul. But it was better than seeing her drift slowly from his life, her eyes darkening with pain and fear every time he walked out the door to do the job he had chosen. He had to make her see she must walk

away now, for he couldn't make himself turn from her
even though he knew he should. From somewhere
deep inside he dragged up enough irritation to make
his voice harsh. "Lady, you are a walking invitation."

Tracy pulled herself out of his arms. "That's a rotten thing to say. I think you had better go." Tracy rose
from the couch, no longer able to stand being so close
to Jon.

Jon got to his feet, hating the anger building between them, hating causing her pain but knowing no
other way to accomplish what he had to do. "Damn
it, I care about you. Can't you see that? I don't want
to see you hurt. I have enough on my conscience
without adding you to the list."

"You let me worry about me. You take care of
yourself."

He took a step toward her, wanting to shake some
sense into her. She glared at him, not backing down an
inch. He stopped, scowling. "Look, can't we talk like
adults? I didn't mean that the way it sounded." At this
moment, he needed her out of his personal life but he
didn't want her angry when he left. She was making
him wish he could be different. "I meant that you are
a giving woman, made for loving. That wasn't an insult, it was a compliment."

As swiftly as her temper caught fire it died. "It
sounded as though you think I'm trying to trap you
into a permanent relationship. I'm not."

Jon searched her face, wanting to believe, knowing
he was a fool for even listening. "What are you sug-
gesting? That we go on as we have?"

"Why not?" she challenged him. Tracy couldn't believe what she was saying. Never in her life had she laid so much of herself and her heart on the line. "Neither of us have anyone else, and we can give each other pleasure. There are no secrets left to hurt us. Why not take what we have and enjoy it?" She planted her hands on her hips, determined to make him hear her.

Jon felt tension ease from his body. His relief was making him light-headed. The past eased its grip, then it slowly slid away. He fought the grin struggling to form on his lips. The situation was too important for humor. He tried to concentrate on her offer but all he could see was her belligerent stance and the fire in her eyes. A chuckle bubbled up before he could catch it. Tracy's glare deepened and she took a menacing step in his direction.

Jon held his position even when her hand came up. "Don't take a swing at me." He laughed, suddenly feeling good. He had thought he would lose her. He had felt the wolf of loneliness breathing down his neck.

"Give me one good reason why I shouldn't, you big ox," she demanded suspiciously. His amusement was contagious. Already she could feel her mood lighten. He wasn't going to push her away. He would let her love him, although she could not say the words. Healing replaced pain. Hope replaced despair. She wanted to wrap her arms around him and not let go.

"Because, despite your less than loverlike delivery, I think I'm going to bow to your judgment instead of my own." This time it was he who moved. He caught her arms and draped them around his neck before

drawing her body against his. Only to himself would
he admit how relieved he was that his tactics for driving her away had failed. He wanted her warmth and
loving more than he had wanted anything in a long
time. And for a while she had chosen to be his.
Knowing him for what he was and what he could not
be, she still wanted him. "Now kiss me and let me love
you. We both need each other. For now or for who
knows how long. Let's enjoy ourselves. You quit remembering and so will I."

Tracy felt his warmth embrace her. She did need
him; to hear him say he needed her was a surprise.
"I've forgot how," she murmured.

His head dipped to catch her words. "Forgot
what?"

"How to enjoy myself," she admitted huskily. He
smelled so good—all man and yet more. His muscles
rippled against her with every movement, calling to
her body to move with him. She arched her hips,
creating an intimacy out of an embrace.

"I'm not sure I remember, either. Do you think we
can struggle along together?" His lips nibbled hers.
Her taste was sweet on his tongue. He wanted more.

"We can try." She stroked his cheek with one hand,
feeling the rasp of his beard. Her palms were too sensitive to the brush of the dark stubble. A shiver ran
over her skin as she moved closer.

He traced a path of kisses down the side of her neck
before touching his lips to the hollow of her throat.
Tracy reacted to the caress as though she were starved
for his touch. She moaned softly, twisting in his arms.
Her hands slid down, exploring his body, pleasuring
him.

"I want you," he breathed against her ear.

"I'm here." She raised her head, her eyes half-closed with the passion he had stoked to flame.

"Your bed isn't." He bent, lifting her in his arms. "And I'm too old for the floor."

She laughed softly, her fingers stroking a part of his anatomy that had no knowledge of age. "Are you? I never would have guessed."

"Witch." He stopped on the stairs to kiss her, delving deep into the mouth that could torment, rage and whisper erotic words with equal abandon.

Tracy took all that he gave, demanding more. She needed him closer than nature could allow them to be. "Did I cast a spell on you?" Her eyes glittered with challenge as he laid her on her bed, his arms caging her had she wanted to escape.

"What do you think? My mind says run as fast and as far as I can from you. But still I stay." The defeat and triumph in his words were somehow a complement to each other.

"I wanted to run, too. But it wouldn't have worked. Your image would have followed me." She unbuttoned his shirt, ignoring the gun that was still strapped to his shoulder.

He shrugged out of his jacket and started to reach for his holster.

"Let me." Tracy smiled as her fingers slid beneath the soft leather and eased it from his shoulder. "I'm not afraid of what you do, I told you that. I could make you a promise that I never will be, but we're not playing a forever game."

Jon felt something inside him shatter at the quiet way she spoke, at the serenity in her eyes as she laid his weapon on the table near her head. The first time she had reached for his gun, he had thought that passion had driven her. This time he knew differently. "You could almost make me believe in forever."

She shook her head, still smiling. "Only for tonight if you like. Tomorrow we'll both be sane again." She pulled off his shirt and tossed it on the floor.

"No forevers." He lifted her in his arms to strip her blouse and bra from her body. Her breasts seemed to rise to meet his hands as he cupped them gently, his thumbs rubbing softly over the taut tips.

"We know better."

Jon bent his head, taking her breast into his mouth. Her groan of pleasure was soft and wild. His body tightened, recognizing its mate. "I can't be slow," he whispered roughly against her tender skin.

"I don't want you to be," Tracy whispered back, lifting her head to nip at his lips. She wanted to drive him wild. She needed to feel him tremble against her, so lost in his passionate need of her that he forgot all the reasons they should not be together. Her hands reached for him as his mouth closed over hers, cupping him, drawing him nearer the union they craved. She arched, teasing him with her hips, attacking then retreating. His moan as he caught her hips, holding her captive, was a man's cry of triumph. She smiled as he thrust into her, meeting the devil of need in his eyes with her own brand of enchantment.

"You can only take what you can keep," she breathed, meeting him stroke for stroke. The heat was building in her and she fought it down. This was no moment for tenderness. The time to burn the bridges to the past had come. The future might hold more sorrow than she could bear, but she would have this night and as many more as she could wrest from fate.

"Is that a challenge?" Jon froze above her, fighting the needs of his body to understand the demands of his mind.

"It's a dare." She wrapped her arms around his neck and drew him down before he could put more words between them. "Accept it if you can."

"You don't fight fair," he rasped as her satiny flesh tightened around him until he lost control.

"I never said I would," she whispered as they hurtled over the edge of desire into the well of fulfillment. She was drowning in heat and pleasure, her limbs weighted and yet light. Darkness hid shadows and her love was stronger than she had known it could be. She might lose but she would fight with fire and passion until she had no more strength to enter the fray.

Chapter 11

The cop was still with Tracy. Bo had been waiting outside her house for two hours and the cop's car hadn't moved. Bo knew what they were doing. The cop was supposed to be chasing him. She was supposed to be worrying about when he would call next. Right now neither was remembering he existed. His anger deepened. His head ached, his hands itched to lay the next set of charges. But he had to wait. The time was not right.

Frustrated, he glared at the house that stood sheltered under the trees. Tracy and the cop shouldn't be sleeping when he was alone and without a place to call his own. Releasing the brake on his car, he let it roll down the hill until it was far enough away that he could start it without being heard.

Tracy snuggled closer to Jon, smiling in her sleep as his body adjusted to her new position. A loud ring disturbed her slumber. Without opening her eyes, she groped for the alarm as Jon stirred groggily beside her. He swore on remembering he wasn't in his own bed.

"You need a longer bed," he muttered.

Tracy opened her eyes as the ringing continued. "I think it's the phone." she pulled herself up and reached for the receiver. A second later she was wide-awake.

"Who is this?" she demanded automatically, knowing the answer.

"Bo. I know you have that cop there with you," he whispered.

Jon heard the angry note in her voice, felt the tension in her body. He slid closer so that he could hear the person on the phone. He wrapped an arm around Tracy's waist, cradling her close as she leaned against him.

"How do you know?" If she hadn't had Jon beside her she wouldn't have been able to keep her panic at bay. Having Bo contact her at the radio station was inconvenient and very unnerving. But having him call her here, where she should have been safe, was terrifying.

"I've been watching you. And you know it, too. That's why *he's* there. Did you think I would hurt you? I won't. I promise. So send him away."

She glanced at Jon for a clue as to how to handle the ultimatum.

"Keep him talking," he mouthed. Finally the tap-and-trace might pay off.

"How do I know you're telling me the truth?" Tracy challenged, not at all sure she was saying the right thing.

"You want proof?" He thought a minute. "All right. I'll give you proof. I set the fires. You wanted to know that. You wanted me to admit it."

"What do you want with me?"

"I . . . I . . ." He paused, floundering for an answer. He wanted her to understand, but it was too soon to tell her why he had come. "Just get rid of the cop. I'll tell you when I know he's gone."

"No!" Tracy felt Jon's surprise at her response! The request was unexpected so she reacted out of emotion rather than logic. "I will not be dictated to. You called me. I don't even know you."

Jon covered the phone with his hand. "Don't scare him away," he commanded roughly, hating to put her through this but having no alternative. It wasn't the first time he'd had to subject someone he had come to know to the grueling moments of dealing with a criminal mind. But it was the first time he had ever felt as though his insides were being ripped out with every change of expression, every quiver of fear, every carefully thought-out word.

"You'd better listen to me," Bo threatened.

Angry, cornered and no longer caring about the fires, Tracy hit back. The firebug's behavior was bordering on intimacy. "Or you'll do what? Burn my house down? If you've been watching, you know you wouldn't be costing me much. I'd get more from the insurance company than this house is worth on the market right now."

"No. No! I wouldn't do that to you. I like you." He was breathing hard, perspiring heavily. "I wasn't trying to frighten you, truly."

"Then Jon stays," she pressed.

"You want him?" He hated the idea but he needed her.

"I do."

He held the phone tightly, angry, confused and hating himself. He didn't want to hurt anyone. There had been enough of that. He wanted justice. "All right. But he won't catch me."

With the last words he hung up. Tracy dropped the receiver in its cradle and started to shake as reaction set in. Where she had gotten the nerve to challenge Bo was beyond her. Jon drew her into his arms, his hands rubbing the tense muscles of her back. If it had been up to him, he would have stopped Tracy's involvement right here.

"Take it easy, honey. It's all right. I'm here." Holding her snug against him with one arm, he reached for the phone with the other. A second later he snapped a demand at the person who answered. His curse followed the response he received. Bo hadn't stayed on the phone long enough for the trace to work. Although they knew there might be other calls, they weren't getting close enough to an answer.

Tracy hardly heard Jon. She was too caught up in the emotional backlash of finding herself vulnerable in her own home. Suspecting that Bo was the prowler who had been stalking her, and then discovering that her feelings were real, was more frightening than she would ever have believed. "Damn. He scares me. A funny little scratchy voice on the phone and he frightens me so badly I can't quit trembling." She nestled closer to Jon. She needed his strength, his warmth and his ability to make her believe things would be all right.

Jon held her closer, feeling her need and responding to it. She was all woman in his arms. Strong when she had to be, facing a danger she had never experienced with courage and I'll-be-damned-if-I'll-let-him-win determination, yet not afraid to turn in Jon's arms and admit her fear. He bent his head, nuzzling at her ear. He meant only to comfort, but her blind seeking of his mouth stole what little of his control remained. His sanity took a nosedive into a limitless well of passion. Tracy twisted in his arms, her hands pulling at him, binding him to her as though she would never let him go.

"What you do to me, woman," he whispered huskily as he laid her back on the bed.

Tracy looked into his eyes, saw his need to hold back. But she didn't care. This minute the future was a vision she had no wish to see. Now was here in his arms. "I want you." She arched her hips, demanding his possession. Slipping her arms around his neck she pulled him down to her, welcoming his weight as another tie to bind them.

"Slowly," Jon commanded, stunned at the power driving her.

"No!" Tracy took his mouth, stopping his protests as he joined them together. Her gasp of pleasure was shared, his breath to hers.

Their mating was a wild force that caught them without defense. Jon thrust deep, she yielded, sheathing him so tightly that pain was a mere breath away. Then he felt release, blessed ease that fed his hunger, driving him deeper yet again. Advance, retreat, harder, faster. The cycle grew stronger with each push, their voices rough with passion and the sharp edge of fulfillment so close and yet so far.

Jon rose high, pulling her hips up for one last stroke. Tracy gasped out his name as the summit was reached. He watched her come apart in his hands just before his own release was granted. With a groan he collapsed on her, his head cushioned on her breasts.

Tracy lay beneath him, breathing heavily, being crushed but not minding. The fear was gone, burned away by their passion. Love. The word quivered on her tongue. She bit it back. Jon was no nearer to being ready to hear her than he had been before. She accepted that just as she accepted the fact that she had green eyes. She had always believed she couldn't trust, and knew now that she did. She was risking everything on a future that was possible only in her dreams.

"Are you all right?" Jon raised his head, surprised at the strange expression on Tracy's face. She was looking at him as though staring into the future. She hadn't heard him, he realized, watching her. The remnants of passion faded from his mind. He could feel himself withdrawing but he fought the urge. They had come through fire together. He could not risk losing whatever time they had left. He propped himself up on his elbows.

Tracy blinked, focusing on his face. The look she saw there told her he was fighting his need to pull away. The pain slipped in her heart even as she eased her arms from his body. She wanted to hold him until he understood she would not follow the path of those who'd destroyed themselves because of his work. She wanted to make him believe in her love and look into his own heart to find love for her waiting there.

"I'm going to check outside. I'll leave Hand on guard by your door until I get back. Try to sleep. I won't disturb you. I'll take the guest room tonight because I want to be able to get up and check the yard at different times. We might get lucky." He watched her closely, expecting an argument. He felt like a heel for leaving her, despite the fact that he had partially told the truth. Just not the greater part. "Are you all right?"

"I'm fine." Her eyes were dry though there were tears in the dark corners of her mind.

Jon frowned, confused at the quiet acceptance in her voice. She had to know what he was feeling, and yet she had let him go easily. She acted as though it was nothing to her that he would leave her arms immediately. He felt guilt, curiosity, bewilderment, a tangle of emotions that had no answers. He shook his head, trying to clear a path to a solution. "I need to keep watch. If I stay here with you I won't be able to keep my mind on the job."

Tracy watched him stand and reach for his slacks on the floor beside the bed. "I understand," she murmured, hearing more than she suspected Jon even knew he was betraying.

She was too calm. Another woman would have been swearing at him, not studying him so carefully, so quietly. Until now nudity had never bothered him. He reached for the sheet and pulled it over Tracy's beautifully relaxed body. "Aren't you cold?"

"You made me warm." She smiled, not sure what she was doing but unable to deny the need to disturb him.

Tracy leaned over the edge of the bed, paying no attention to the sheet as she lifted his shirt and rolled onto her back to hand it to him. Her breasts lay above the edge of the sheet. She watched his eyes trace their fullness, saw him wince as though in pain.

"Don't do this to me." He groaned, sitting beside her on the bed. His fingers raised, gently outlined the peaks, and he saw the nipples harden in response.

"What am I doing? I'm not the one sending you away."

"I can't stay."

"Why?" She held her breath in an agony of hope.

He was hurting. Didn't she see that? Her scent was all around, drawing him into a silken trap. Her body was a piece of heaven on earth. Her mind was an elusive puzzle that would never grow old. Her passion warmed him, driving out the loneliness that haunted him.

"I can't give you more than I am now." The words were drawn from him in invisible blood.

"You won't give me more," she corrected, studying every expression on his face. Her future was at stake. "I'm willing to take the risk."

"You don't know what it's like. You talk about taking a risk based on what you think, not on the reality."

"Give me a chance."

"No, damn it!" He rose. To stay was to hold heaven and watch it turn to a living hell. "I won't. I can't have your promises of forever and then give you up when you need to leave. And you will want that one day. I don't know anyone who survives intact." He turned and started for the door.

"Everyone changes. It's part of life," Tracy whispered the words, knowing they would make no difference. She couldn't force him to take her gift.

"It also can be part of death. I won't be responsible for that for you or for myself. Because of you I question myself and my work. That increases my danger, because a distracted mind is one that makes mistakes. You matter to me, too much. I won't lie to you about that, but I don't have a death wish. Right now, I can see you hurting. I need to be on guard tonight and you have every right to expect me to share your bed. I want to. But I won't. One little thing and you're hurting already. For now, we both can pay the price of being together, but what of a year from now? People like Bo are a part of my life. If I share my life with you they become a part of yours. Right now, I hate the fact that you're dealing with this nut. I've never felt this way before. I don't want to feel this way now. Can't you understand? I find I'm selfish. I can't bear watching you learn to be afraid, to feel you drawing away because you've learned the meaning of regret and pain." He kept his back to her as he spoke.

Hearing the finality in his voice, Tracy played her only card. "I love you."

He tensed. He hadn't thought she would say it. "Maybe you do but I won't love you." Her gasp of pain was soft, going through him like a knife. He walked out then, hating himself because he would not fight for her.

Tracy lay back on the pillows, feeling more alone than she ever had in her life. There was no future because Jon had decreed it. Anger would have helped but she just couldn't find it in her heart to feel the emotion. Jon was paying a high price to walk away. Another man would have taken what she offered and not counted the cost for either of them.

She knew then she would not give up. Jon had given her more in the past few minutes than all the hours he had spent in her arms. A man did not bare his soul to a woman unless there was more than chemistry between them. He had admitted to caring, one step closer to loving. She had to remember that. It was the one star in the emotional darkness of the night. As long as there was life there was hope he would grow to love her. She had to believe that.

Jon rolled on his back, glared up at the darkened ceiling and damned himself for acting like a fool. There were a hundred ways a man could be an idiot around a woman and he had found a new one tonight. She loved him and he wasn't going to do a thing about it. Statistics didn't lie. His past didn't lie. His eyes and ears didn't betray him. His career had terrible side effects. He couldn't, he wouldn't put any woman through such pain again.

The average relationship had plenty going against it for the moment, but his life-style was at the top of the list of risky choices. He had other options but so far he had found nothing could change his mind. Tracy made him doubt himself and he didn't like that. There were few enough people willing to try to make a difference when criminals roamed the streets almost at will, when the courts paid more attention to the criminals' rights than to the victims', when society itself condoned drugs, drunks, con men and liars. When stealing from the government was an example of the big guy getting his just deserts and arson wasn't much of a crime because there were so many bigger things going on: murder, rape, drug deals and gang wars. He was a fighter, not as often on the front line since he had discovered solving a crime was more challenging for him than catching the criminal.

He kicked back the covers and let the air-conditioning drift across his heated skin. Tracy made him forget his need to make a difference. Without conceit, he knew he was good at his work. He knew he was regarded as something of a throwback to another time by the men he worked with. He still believed in honor, respect for property and life and truth. Patriotism and law weren't just words to him. He lived them. He breathed them regardless of whether the rest of the world valued his ideas.

Knowing he would be unable to sleep, Jon rose and paced to the window. The intracoastal was dark, silent. The shadows probably hid more than one drug boat on its way to or from a deal. The cargo would be on the streets in less than forty-eight hours. Every night, he went to sleep with that kind of knowledge on his mind. He knew how often rapes occurred in the United States, how many minutes between murders, how many millions of dollars insurance companies lost each year to theft, fire and con games. He walked in a world filled with ugliness and shadows—and Tracy would have to share that with him.

He swore with quiet vehemence before turning from the window. The faint moonlight coming through the window illuminated the phone on the bedside stand. Bo *was* the firebug. And now he seemed to be branching into some sort of fixation on Tracy that went beyond her professional life. Jon frowned, thinking about the man hounding Tracy. Jon couldn't face any more thoughts about his future. It would be better to deal with something or someone who had a solution.

He walked to the phone and dialed Doc's private number. Calling people in the middle of the night was becoming a habit, he thought with a grim twist to his lips. A groggy voice answered on the fourth ring. Jon identified himself.

"This better be good, Kent," the psychologist grumbled irritably.

"You're going to have to tell me that," Jon returned, propping pillows behind his head as he lay down. "Tracy just got another call from the firebug tonight. At home."

"What? How'd he get her number? Is she in the directory?"

"She's listed with the operator."

"What happened?"

Jon related the conversation as close to verbatim as possible.

"I don't like the sound of this. The classic profile of a torch is someone who set fires to watch things burn. Frequently he gets his sexual kicks that way. Rarely do you find one of them bothering a woman unless he's showing off. I think we can rule that out in this case, because of the length of time these fires have been going on and the number of locations involved that have nothing to do with Ms. Michaels."

"So give me an opinion as to what this guy is up to. Bo is getting entirely too personal for my peace of mind."

"All I can give you is a guess. From listening to those tapes of his contacts that you sent over, I definitely agree that he has some sort of revenge or retribution motive. And I'm no linguist, but hearing that recording the sound director made removing the distortion, I agree with you that Bo and Ms. Michaels are from the same general location. That fact may be our tie-in regarding why he started contacting her in the first place. He's got to be out there and alone, or *feeling* alone. He probably views Tracy as his personal friend or confidante. You're getting between them, hence his demand for her to send you away. The fact that he backed down indicates that she means something very important to him and that doesn't sound good at all. If he's getting obsessive where she's concerned, he could get dangerous. Especially if he feels her interest is being directed elsewhere. All in all I think we better get him off the streets ASAP. He's deviating too far from the pattern he's established. That rarely means anything but trouble in capital letters."

"I like it when you get so definite." Jon's sarcasm was more a release of his own anger than a dig at the psychologist.

"You know me. I always play it cautious. Maybe that's why we get along so well." He hesitated then asked, "What's the plan? And how's Ms. Michaels handling the situation? It can be terrifying to be the recipient of this kind of obsession. She showed courage standing up to the guy, but is it the kind of arrogance that could get her hurt?"

"I don't think so. She seems to understand the situation and is willing to go along with any measures that ensure her safety. The lady just isn't into someone telling her what she should do." His lips twisted into a reluctant half smile. "She has a mind of her own and a rather unique way of getting what she wants."

The silence between the two men was swift and longer than it should have been.

"This is way out of line, buddy, but if you need to talk, I'm here."

Doc had been counseling police department personnel and their families for many years. Jon had seen him at the time of Amanda's death. Their friendship had been cemented then. "If I thought talking would help I'd tell you to bring your couch. I told her about Amanda."

William waited a moment then added, when nothing was forthcoming from Jon, "How did she take it?"

Jon sighed deeply. "I don't know. Better than I expected, I guess."

"Then what's bothering you? Your reactions? Did you expect her to run? She doesn't sound like a lady who would."

"Maybe I did," Jon admitted.

Doc sighed deeply. "You're one of the strongest men I know but you've got a blind spot where your duty and honor lie. Find that spot and deal with it before it gets so deeply entrenched that you spend your life alone. This woman sounds special to you. Give her and yourself a chance. Take a shot at the future. No one gets guarantees. You know that."

"I can't." The words were drawn from him. "I've spent most of my life alone. Tracy's more important to me than Amanda ever was. I'm thinking about futures now. I don't want to but I can't stop."

"So what's the choice? Watch her walk away and you're still alone."

"But at least she'll be happy."

William made a rude noise. "Maybe, maybe not. In my opinion you don't give the woman much credit. She might be strong enough to take on you, your profession and your solitary existence. She might be just what the doctor ordered to link you with the rest of the human race."

Jon frowned, never having heard his actions put in just those words. "You'd better explain that."

"Even before Amanda you had a detached air about you that everyone who knows you was aware of. Nothing really seemed to bother you. We both know you feel emotion but you don't show it. You can look at things that would send grown men to the bushes getting rid of their lunch, and you don't *see* them. I've watched you and I've watched the men you work with. They're in awe of you. Your control, your ability to think under pressure, your ability to see everything in terms of clues or pieces of a giant picture. You are superb at what you do because you don't let emotion rule your head. But what about your emotional needs? You're denying them. How long can you go on doing that? And at what cost? Everyone needs someone."

Jon turned Doc's words over in his mind. There was truth in them. "You sound like Tracy."

"Then she's one smart lady."

Jon grinned slightly at the complacent tone. "You're an arrogant so-and-so."

"We can't all be perfect, my friend." Doc sobered, returning to the subject that had wakened him in the middle of the night. "And about your firebug, I would say stick close to your lady. This Bo character is on the edge. Control is slipping out of his hands and he's bound to be feeling the heat of his pursuers. He's taking risks that he's never taken before, and he's involving someone who seems to mean something to him. The ingredients are there for a nasty little blowup. Anything could send him over, and you don't want him taking Tracy with him when he goes.''

Chapter 12

Tracy woke to the smell of bacon frying and coffee brewing. She stretched leisurely, in no hurry to leave her bed. Today was Saturday and she wasn't alone. The angle of the sun coming in the windows told her it was late. She wondered vaguely if Jon had passed as difficult a night in the guest room as she had alone in bed. Probably, she decided, slipping from the covers and heading for the bathroom. His conscience had to be giving him hell. Knowing he was hurting caused her pain, but if it gave them a future she wouldn't count the cost to either of them. She showered and dressed, determined to take her cue on how to act from him. She wasn't giving up.

The house was quiet as she descended the stairs. Jon looked up when she entered the kitchen. Nothing in his eyes told her what he thought or even that he remembered the time he had spent in her arms.

"Did you sleep well?" he asked quietly before turning away to pour another cup of coffee.

"No." She saw no point in lying when the vague shadows beneath her eyes would give her away.

"Makes two of us," he admitted, handing her the mug as she joined him at the counter. He watched her face. "I lay awake part of the night thinking about us."

Tracy controlled her surprise at his confession. "Did you? What was the conclusion?" She took a sip of coffee, working at being as calm as Jon. All she could remember was the sight of his back as he walked away from her despite hearing her say she loved him.

"I think I'm a fool."

"If you're expecting an argument, you won't get it."

He laughed humorlessly. "Don't you want to know why?"

She delayed answering by taking another swallow of coffee. His voice didn't give her much hope even if his words should have. "If you want to tell me." She still wasn't certain she had made the right decision in telling him that she loved him.

Jon stared at her, not believing she was the same woman he had held in his arms, the same woman who had given him more pleasure than he had ever known. This one was too indifferent, too controlled. The passion that should have been in her eyes was replaced with wary curiosity. Suddenly he was angry. Angry that that he had walked away from her, angry that she had let him and angry that she could stand beside him drinking coffee as though they had never been lovers. He didn't need anyone to tell him his reactions were extreme. He plucked the cup from her hand when she would have brought it to her lips again. He dropped both mugs on the counter and pulled her into his arms.

Startled, Tracy opened her lips to protest. His tongue invaded before she could get the words out. She tried to fight him but lost the battle almost before it had begun. He held her tight against his body, using the counter to provide the second half of the trap. His hands stroked her back, settling at the base of her spine to tip her hips into his. He raised his head to glare at her. Her taste was in his mouth and her scent was wrapped around him, stirring the desire he barely had leashed.

"All right, woman. I can't fight you any longer. I don't even want to try. I can't forget my past. I want to but I can't. Can you take a chance on me the way I am?"

If Tracy had been a woman who could only love with hearts-and-flowers romance she would have cried at the harshly spoken demand. Instead, all she felt was the heady delight that he was letting her into his life. "Do you think you would be here now if I weren't willing to take a chance? I can understand about Amanda and your child. I would probably even feel the same way were I in your shoes. But there are no guarantees in life. Your work worries me. I won't pretend it doesn't. But I believe in myself enough to know I won't cave in at the first sign of trouble or danger. I won't dump my emotions in your lap and expect you to deal with them. I won't trap you with guilt and I won't hide my tears. I'll give you honesty." She lifted her hand to touch the deeply etched lines on his brow and at the corners of his mouth. His thoughts in the night had been no kinder to him than hers. He looked tired, worn and infinitely appealing.

Jon stared into her eyes, wanting to believe in her more than he had wanted anything in his life. "And if we can't make it?"

"Then I'll walk away."

"Hurting." His voice was harsh with the price he would pay at knowing he caused her pain.

"I'll survive." Tracy held him to her, absorbing his resistance. "You aren't responsible for me. I am. It's my choice to decide on the risks I think acceptable."

Jon stared at her, trying to gauge the strength of her determination. She met his eyes without hesitation. Her courage was a bright banner that was marked by the delicate thrust of her chin, the I-can-do-anything expression. He wanted her. He didn't trust her love, he wasn't even sure he trusted himself. But he wanted her—on any terms.

"All right." He touched her face, tracing the slender bones there until his fingers brushed her lips. "I'll try to trust but the odds are against us."

Tracy relaxed, warmed by his effort and his touch. "I've seen worse. And trying is enough for now."

He released his breath with a deep sigh. "If you believe nothing else, believe that I *want* to trust us." He bent his head to take her mouth. Her kiss was sweet, easing the confusion and the pain of uncertainty.

Tracy held nothing back. She wanted him to know she needed him. She wanted him to learn he needed her in ways that were as important as the passion and the fire they shared.

Jon raised his head, a smile curving his lips. "So, lady of mine, what do we do today?"

"It's such a nice day I had intended to start clearing away some of the debris in the yard."

Jon watched her, certain she was joking. "I don't have much experience in that area," he said when he realized she was serious. "I've always lived in apartments."

"Then you're in for an interesting day. You haven't lived until you've tackled my house. It has a way of separating the weak from the strong and destroying any illusions about a person's manual dexterity." She grinned, suddenly conscious that the day seemed brighter. "But not in these clothes."

Jon glanced down at himself. "Last night I didn't come prepared to move in," he murmured dryly. "After breakfast we could go back to my apartment and pick up some things."

"You can. I'll stay here."

He shook his head before she could finish speaking. "Nothing doing. We stick together until Bo is caught. One of the things I meant to talk to you about this morning is your admirer." He picked up their mugs, emptied the now cold coffee in the sink and poured each a fresh cup. "If you'll set the table I'll see to the eggs."

Tracy took her cup, carrying it with her to the linen drawer. It was easier to be calm about Bo in the light of day. "What about my admirer?"

Jon watched her take place mats from the cabinet. "No comments about my taking on the chore of cook?" He cocked a brow, curious at her answer.

"I don't like cooking in the morning." She shrugged, giving him an unrepentant grin.

He had to share her amusement. The day was proceeding much better than he could have hoped. "For that I ought to dish up a mess of scrambled eggs, but I think I'll treat you to a herb omelet instead."

"And an explanation about Bo."

He sobered immediately. "And him." He set out the skillet and collected a carton of eggs from the refrigerator. "I called the department psychologist last night after I left you."

Startled, Tracy paused in the act of laying the silverware. "He must have loved you getting him out of bed at that hour."

"Not exactly, but it wasn't the first time. Anyway, I told him about your call. He thinks this guy may be flipping over the edge in his behavior toward you. Neither of us like the personal overtones in his response to knowing you and I are together."

Tracy returned to her job, her brow furrowed in thought. "You think Bo will keep contacting me."

"Don't you?"

"I don't know why he did in the first place."

"A touch of home, perhaps. I know you listened to that tape Walter set up for us without the distortion in Bo's voice. You heard the same kind of accent in his speech that comes out in yours."

The phone rang, interrupting them. Tracy looked at it as if it were a snake in her kitchen. Jon moved to her side, urging her without words to lift the receiver. She almost collapsed against his chest on hearing Roger's voice on the other end of the line.

"Yeah, what is it?" Jon demanded, taking the receiver and wrapping his arm around Tracy's waist.

"I got that list of employees we talked about, starting with the first fire set in Virginia more than two years ago. There isn't a single name that appears everywhere, but there are one or two that pop up in more than a few. But none of the matches are in the same state. And none have the same social security number—some are similar but not the same."

Jon considered the information, not liking the questions it raised. "This guy is smart. I'll bet he's leaving a trail of aliases and bogus social security numbers behind. Leave the list on my desk. I'll stop by the station this morning to look it over. Anything else?"

"That's it for now."

Jon hung up and turned Tracy in his arms. "Are you all right?"

She nodded. "I think I need to get a bit more like you. Every time that phone rings I expect it to be Bo." She shuddered at the thought.

"We'll get him. I promise you. We're beginning to narrow the field a little. Hooking the fires together up the east coast to Virginia was a stroke of luck. Now Roger has a list of the employees at each target that didn't check out. We're narrowing the field."

"I heard." Tracy leaned her head against his chest, allowing herself the luxury of relying on his strength for a moment.

Jon looked down at her, curled so trustingly against him and knew that the hardest thing he would ever do would be to walk away from her. With every moment he spent with her, he learned how lonely he had been. His arms tightened around her even as he fought the old need to pull away. He had promised her that he would give them a chance, that he would try trusting her.

"Come on, let's eat or you and your yard aren't going to get the benefit of my dubious talents in debris clearing."

"You may regret this," she felt compelled to warn.

"Probably, but that won't stop me." He set her away and returned to the stove.

The next two hours passed rapidly. They started with breakfast and followed that up with a trip to Jon's apartment where he packed an overnight bag. The stop at the police station took longer than anticipated, because Roger had somehow managed to hook into a computer and come up with a list of all the social security numbers on the employment records of the burned-out businesses, and the names they were supposed to belong to. He hadn't had a chance to compare the two sheets before Jon arrived.

Jon studied the printouts, frowning at the numbers in front of him. Suddenly, his gaze sharpened. "Roger, look at this one guy. I don't think the numbers are totally phony. But the damn digits have been completely rearranged. Look, every one of these sets has exactly the same numbers in the group. I bet the odds on that are right off the scale." Working quickly, Jon lined up the numbers. "Also look at this list of names. Brian Long. Bert Logan. Buster Lister. Barney Lyle. Bob Little. There's a B.L. on each employment list. Want to bet this is Bo? Want to bet that somewhere in this list of aliases is Bo's real name? Start with that Bob Little you found the first day. Run these numbers through the computer with all the possible combinations until you get a match between the numbers and the aliases. If he used the same initials each time, it stands to reason he might have done the same with the social security number. Once we have the name and the number, we're on our way."

Roger frowned down at the sheet as he muttered a curse. "I should have seen that."

Jon got to his feet. "Don't worry about it. You're the one who got the information. I just pieced it together." He headed for the door. "I'll be at Tracy's. Call me there as soon as you get the answer."

Roger looked up, his eyes shrewd. "I get the feeling that there's something more than guard duty going on with you two."

"Sort of."

Roger chuckled at the evasive answer. "You don't give much away, my friend. You better watch out or she might just change that little trait of yours."

Jon scowled. "Stick to your work, microchip whiz. One of these days your turn will come." He turned, moving toward the door.

"Don't count on it," Roger called after him, adding, "You can't leave me with this. I canceled a date last night to get this stuff together. You can't expect me to slave around here all day while you're off enjoying yourself."

"I won't be enjoying myself exactly. I'm going to be chopping trees or something equally obnoxious."

Roger's mouth dropped open. "You're kidding."

Jon laughed at his shocked expression. "Nope. Not a bit. When you see me Monday I'll have calluses on my hands and probably more aches and pains than I deserve." Jon strolled out of the station, feeling a sense of satisfaction at not only finding a possible break in the case but also giving Roger a dose of his own medicine.

Tracy watched him walk toward her, wondering what had put him in such a good mood. She asked as soon as he joined her in the car.

Not wanting to raise her hopes, he confined his response to the second reason for his mood. "I just gave ol' Roger a shock. I can't think how many times I've covered for him when he had a date. Now the shoe is on the other foot and he doesn't like it one bit." He started the car, feeling a definite surge of male superiority. Roger had been fairly scathing about Tracy before he had met her. But Jon had noticed that a very interested look had made its appearance when Roger was introduced to her. Jon had no doubt that Roger would have gladly changed places with him, even to the point of taking up a shovel.

"I never expected you to work all day," Tracy said as she joined Jon on the steps of the back porch.

Jon opened one eye without moving from his reclining position against one of the columns. Every muscle in his body protested the unaccustomed activity. He had thought himself in shape and had learned differently. He was hot, tired and sweaty. He wanted a bed and a shower in that order. What he got was a concerned look on the face of an angel as she took a seat beside him. His aches eased with her closeness.

"Every time I thought about stopping I looked around and realized I couldn't leave the stuff I could see needed doing," he admitted ruefully. His glance shifted from her face to the now cleared yard, the scrubbed flagstone path leading to the water's edge.

His hands were as rough as that path but not nearly as clean. His original intent had been only to help her. Somewhere along the way he had gotten caught up in her enthusiasm to turn the uncared-for house and property into a home.

Tracy turned to look over her yard. With Jon's help she had accomplished in a day what would have taken her a week or more to do alone. She glanced at him, taking in the scrapes on his knuckles, the dirt on his legs below the cutoff jeans and the chest glistening with sweat revealed by the half-open shirt stretched across his shoulders.

"Do you like what you see?"

Tracy lifted her eyes to his, seeing desire for the first time that day. The late-afternoon sun flickered through the trees, touching him with golden light. "Too much for my peace of mind."

The sun was cool compared to the heat of her gaze. "I shouldn't be interested in making love to you. I ache in places that have nothing to do with passion. I need a bath and I want you right now. On this damn hard porch, in broad daylight where anyone coming by could see us and interrupt. I haven't felt like this since I was a teenager." He lifted his hand to cup her cheek. "Tell me to stop."

"How? I'm in no better shape. I want you, too. And you aren't the only one who needs a bath." She smiled because listening to him was the easiest thing she had ever done. The sun was warm on her back, a faint breeze was whispering through the trees and all around them was silence. The world was waiting.

"Then let's solve at least one problem and clean up together." His other hand came up to frame her face.

Drawing her gently toward him, he tasted her mouth, nibbling at her lips, teasing them open.

"Kiss me," Tracy demanded when he played rather than possessed. She wanted him close, hard against her.

"You kiss me," he returned huskily. She felt good in his arms. Soft, sweet and all female. He hadn't known he could feel so primitive with a woman. She was his. A piece of his dreams and the heart of his reality. What if they couldn't make the future work? A shudder went through him at the thought. He had spent his life in danger of one sort or another. He had faced a gun pointed at his gut with more courage than he faced the vision of a tomorrow without Tracy in it.

Tracy felt his shudder as her own body trembled in anticipation. In Jon's arms she could forget about Bo, the fires and the possible danger in which she stood. All she wanted was Jon's touch, the feel of his body joined with hers and the pleasure he brought her. Taking his face in her hands she kissed him, her tongue delving deep to take all he would give and more. When his arms came around her, she groaned huskily, feeling desire tightening within her.

Fighting to raise his head, Jon finally succeeded. "I said kiss me, not burn me alive," he said hoarsely.

"You don't like?"

"Too much, lady with the torch, but I don't want to make love to you right here." He pulled one of her hands down to rest on the evidence of just how much she aroused him. "I'm filthy."

She laughed. "I would have said earthy." This time her kiss held more mischief than passion. She jumped to her feet and ran into the house calling, "The last one out of the tub is a rotten egg."

Jon stared after her, unprepared for her flight. A slow grin built. He knew which one of them would be the last one out. "So you like to play games, do you, lover," he murmured, getting to his feet. "I know some games you'll really like."

Bo frowned watching the one called Kent move deliberately up the back steps to the door. Time was running out for all of them. Tonight was almost the last job. One more after this one. Then he would tell the world why, through Tracy. But first he had to figure a way. Kent was a danger to him. It had taken some digging, but the knowledge of the street he had gained over the past two years had given him a source for information. He knew all about Kent. His ability to solve problems that usually went unsolved, his ability to track a man until he caught him. Kent never gave up. How many times had he heard that? He had to stay one step ahead of the man to win. He couldn't take the cop out because he was no killer. But Tracy wouldn't give him up and he needed Tracy. So he was stuck.

Bo shook his head and backed into the trees. Now that they had cleared the property, there was no longer any cover to allow him to get as close as he wanted. He had to think, to plan. Tonight was the next hit. The thought brought a grim smile to his face as he exited the trees and got into a pale beige car. The seats were hot, the interior a minihell. He didn't notice the sweat or the bugs. All he could see was one more name crossed off his list. One more debt paid in kind.

Chapter 13

Night crept slowly over the intracoastal. Tracy stood at the living room window watching the sky darken. Jon wrapped his arms around her waist and drew her back against him.

"That was Roger."

"What did he say?"

"He's been running nine numbers in all their combinations as social security numbers and then matching each one with the list of names that we think are Bo's aliases."

"I don't understand." Tracy frowned, seeing Jon's face in the glass. The light from the room outlined them both, heightening the aura of intimacy.

"The way we figure it, Bo has been getting some kind of temporary employment in each company that burned, so he can case the building. He comes in under a fictitious name and a doctored social security number, because every personnel office now requires those numbers. He works just long enough to find out about alarms and security measures and then quits. A few days later—we aren't exactly sure of the time schedule yet—he sets his little bombs and another business bites the dust. We've got another team also looking farther back in employment records, trying to find a tie-in for a motive, either retribution or revenge connected with Bo himself or someone close to him. That investigation isn't going as well.''

"It's like a maze," she said, impressed by the amount of tedious work involved. "I had no idea."

"Few people do. Law enforcement is seen as a very physical existence. For the most part it isn't." Jon sighed as he rested his chin on her hair. Holding her was becoming as necessary to him as breathing. Telling her about his work was easier with each day. He was coming to depend on her in his life, and he no longer fought the growing need.

"So what happens now?"

"We wait. This has been hard on you right from the beginning. If we'd been able to convince that judge to let us tap the call-in line at the radio station, we might have Bo already." This time Jon's sigh held disgust and acceptance. "But that would have meant an invasion of privacy for a lot of innocent people. So you and I wait. Bo's out there and he'll call again. Things are coming to a head."

"I feel it, too. I wonder what his reason is." She leaned back, resting against Jon. "With as much trouble as he has gone to, it has to be a powerful one." She turned in his arms. "I wonder how long it will take to get over the feeling of being watched?"

"A while maybe." He hauled her close, watching the window as she had done. He wanted to give her back her ordinary life. He wanted to promise her that she wouldn't remember the fear and the anger. He knew better than to try. He could only hold her when she needed him and give what comfort he could as they waited for the end to come.

The phone rang on the bedside stand. Tracy rolled over and grabbed for it, the sound bringing her instantly awake.

"It's time for another one."

She sat up, recognizing Bo's voice. She felt Jon sit up beside her, but she concentrated on the phone and the clock. She had to keep Bo on the line for at least three minutes. "Another what?"

"Another fire. Tonight. I wanted you to know. There'll be one more after this one, and then I'll be done."

Her brows rose at the startling pronouncement. "Why?"

"Justice."

"For whom?"

Bo hesitated. He wanted to tell her now, but he didn't dare go through the story before the last job. They would stop him. He couldn't have that. He frowned, trying to remember something else. Lately, it was hard to remember some things. He shook his head to clear it. "I'll tell you next time, after the last fire." Now he remembered. He had to watch the time. The police did things like trace calls. The cop was there with her right now. "Tell Kent he won't get me before

I'm done. I want justice and we both know that doesn't happen in real life. Ask Kent.''

Tracy stared at the phone angrily buzzing out a dial tone. ''He hung up. Now he's talking about you as though he knows you.'' She looked at Jon. ''How can he?''

Jon got out of bed and collected his clothes. ''He's probably been asking around. I'm not that invisible on the street. My size alone sees to that. But that's not important right now. You heard him. He's going to set another fire tonight. This time I want to be there.'' He yanked on his pants and shirt.

Tracy got up, pushed by his sense of purpose. ''But what can you possibly do until you know where he's set the fire?''

''For one thing, I can get closer to West Palm Beach. We're at least twenty minutes away. My car has a radio and the minute the alarm sounds at the fire station I'll be able to roll.'' He pulled on his second shoe, glancing at Tracy to find her dressing quickly. ''What the devil are you doing?''

She didn't hesitate. ''Coming with you. Bo dealt me into this and I want to be there with you.''

''No way.'' He started for the door. ''You'll be safer here with the patrol cars watching the house. If you're worried I'll get someone to stay in the house with you.''

''In your dreams,'' she returned smartly, collecting her shoes to hurry after him. ''I won't be in any danger while he's worrying about his fire, and I couldn't have any better protection than being with you.''

Jon stopped, turning so abruptly that Tracy bumped into him before she could help herself.

"I said no and I meant it. I don't have time to argue." He glared at her when she shook her head.

"I won't be left behind. You're wasting time. Let's go." She brushed past him, picking up her purse on the way to the front door.

Jon stalked after her, knowing she was right about one thing. He didn't have time to make her stay. "All right. But you stay in the car when we get there, with the windows rolled up and the doors locked. Understand?"

"I'm not stupid. I'll be careful." She slid into the passenger side of his car.

"No, but I am for letting you bully me into this," he muttered, starting the engine with one hand while switching on the radio with the other. He pulled out of the drive while reporting Bo's phone call to both Roger and the fire department.

Tracy said nothing as she watched the scenery speed by. She felt no fear, because of her trust in Jon's competence to handle whatever situation awaited them.

Bo took a deep breath and set the last charge. Glancing at his watch, he counted the minutes left to get out of the building. A sound alerted him that he was not alone. He whirled as a man came up the stairwell, gun drawn.

"Hold it!"

Bo crouched, swung around, using his knapsack as a weapon. The half-loaded pouch caught the security guard in the chest, knocking the breath out of him in an audible whoosh. Without waiting to see if the man recovered he brushed past and raced for the stairs.

Time was running out. He had to get out of the building, especially get off the roof before the fire began.

He'd made it to the ground floor, near the front door, when the first charge blew at the back of the building. He had ten seconds to get to the street. Breathing heavily, he slammed through the door and into the humid night air. The second explosion was closer. He gained the far side of the road, sliding into the shadow of an office building. The fourth went up. The flames were visible in the front windows. He stopped counting at five, his eyes now on the roof. He could see the guard racing around the perimeter, looking for a way down.

He hadn't meant the man to be hurt, but there was no escape for the guard. To jump meant certain death. To stay was to be caught in the fire eating its way up the walls to the hole that would soon be in the roof. The last explosion was the most powerful of them all. The fire seemed to sense the source of oxygen at the top of the man-made chimney. It raced for the fuel, destroying the destroyer.

Bo watched the orange beast uncurl, roaring with each twist of its body. Justice for a life lost. He pulled the list from his pocket as the sirens screamed in the distance. One red line through the next to the last name: Boyer Associates.

He turned away, already thinking of the building where he had just gotten work as a janitor. He smiled a little at the irony. In all but three cases he had had the same position.

Bo froze then, his smile dying as a car pulled to a halt before the burning building. He recognized the man who got out. The woman stayed in the sedan. The streetlights and the fire illuminated her face clearly.

Tracy. Adrenaline surged at the feel of danger. He had never been so near to detection before. His hands flexed, and his muscles strained at the need to creep closer. The cop turned, his eyes searching the shadows. Bo shrank back as the fire engine arrived, its siren dying with one last shrieking wail. He watched Kent stalk around the car and say something to Tracy through the half-open window. Then the cop left her to join the captain and two other men who'd pulled up in a car similar to Kent's.

He frowned, not liking the fact that Kent had left Tracy alone so close to the building. Already the fire was hot enough to explode the first set of windows. The rain of glass had been light, but it wouldn't stay that way for long. And then there was the danger of the fire spreading. Worried, he edged closer.

Tracy stared at the fire licking at the building like a hungry predator. Jon was too close. He was without the protective gear the fire people wore. Tracy's eyes strained to keep sight of him in the bustle of activity. Hoses were linked and spread to try to control the blaze, to keep it from moving to a building nearby. Suddenly she heard a shout as everyone seemed to freeze for an instant, looking up toward the roof.

"No!" Tracy gazed at the figure frantically waving from the edge of the roof. Had the firebug been caught in his own handiwork? Without thinking she opened the door and got out, her eyes glued to the man silhouetted against the sky.

"They'll get him down."

Startled at the voice at her elbow, Tracy froze. She knew that voice. Bo! Her eyes searched frantically for Jon. What should she do? she wondered. If she turned Bo might run. If she pretended she hadn't recognized his voice, would he stay close without trying to hurt her, or would he talk? Bo seemed calm enough now, almost dispassionate. *Jon,* she begged silently, *come to me.* The smoke billowed before her, men shouted and rushed about. No one noticed her or the man behind her. She was on her own. Gathering her courage in her hands, she tried a desperate gamble.

"How can you be sure?" she asked carefully, still focusing on the trapped man. Maybe he would stay as long as she made no move to entrap him. Maybe Jon would look around and realize that she had company.

"The fire has a few minutes to go before it reaches the roof. It isn't hungry enough yet. There's still some oxygen in the lower levels to feed it."

Tracy frowned at the strange way Bo spoke about the fire. She tried to concentrate on the rescue operation being mounted from the ground rather than turn and confront the man everyone hunted. The ladder truck was moved into position, the firemen mounting its rungs before she would have believed it safe to climb.

"I wonder who's on the roof," Tracy murmured, looking for anything to keep the conversation going. *Jon, where are you?* she called again in her mind. She needed him.

Suddenly, a window exploded, causing a shower of lethal glass. Bo pushed Tracy down behind the shelter of the car. "He's someone who shouldn't have been here. Like you, Miss Michaels."

Tracy turned her head, startled at the rough anger in a voice that had initially been so calm. All she saw was a glimpse of Bo's shadowy figure merging with the darkness of the building at her back.

"Stay down where it's safe before you get hurt," he called softly over his shoulder, not daring to stay even though someone should be with her to protect her.

Shaken at being so close to the firebug, Tracy sagged against the car. Jon found her that way a moment later.

"Are you all right?" He ran his hands over her body as he brought her to her feet. Even in the flickering orange light he could she was pale. "Are you cut? Hurt?" Her dazed eyes frightened him.

"Bo was here," she said. "The firebug. He was here."

Jon stilled, his hands gripping her shoulders. "What do you mean *here*? Did you see him?"

"I talked to him."

"I told you to stay in the car. Where did he go?" He raised his head and shouted for the two detectives who had responded to the fire call. The men came on the run. "Comb the area. Tracy thinks she spoke to the firebug." He glanced at Tracy. "Which way did he head?" he demanded.

Tracy pointed to the building behind them, watching as the pair rushed off.

Jon opened the car door and stuffed her gently inside. "This time stay put until I get back. If you don't I'll paddle your backside until you can't sit down for a week." Whatever Tracy might have said to this masculine threat was lost. Jon was moving away before he finished speaking.

Tracy wrapped her arms around her body to stave off the sudden chills racing over her skin. She had been so close. She should have listened to Jon. The phone calls were bad enough, but being that near to the deranged, angry man responsible for the fires was scarier than she'd ever anticipated. The memory of Bo's calm voice telling her the security guard on the roof would be all right was starkly vivid. He hadn't sounded worried at all. Maybe the police weren't right on the mark about Bo's determination to keep his criminal activities down to bloodless destruction of property. Maybe it was only chance that had given him a clean record to date. Tonight, but for the amazingly swift response time of the fire department and their quick work at getting the man off the roof unharmed, chance could have taken a holiday.

"What did you find, Reese?" Jon demanded.

Reese shook his head as he waited for his partner to show up. "Turk and I split up. I didn't find anything. You?"

"Not a sign of him. It's like he melted into the night," Jon replied, as his eyes swept the area, looking for something, anything, that would give them a clue about the firebug's escape route.

Turk came puffing up, cursing steadily. "I think that idiot took the elevator up to the roof and across the ones to the east until he couldn't go any farther and then dropped to the ground. I found this near the edge of the roof." He held out a small fuse.

Jon took the thin piece, turning it over in his hands before stuffing it in his pocket. "He's making mistakes now," he murmured in satisfaction. "He's getting cocky and he's making mistakes."

"Big deal," Reese snapped. "The rat still gave us the slip."

"He won't the next time," Turk told his partner.

"Now what?" Reese asked, looking at Jon.

"I'm taking Tracy home. You two talk to that guard and see what you can find out. I'll talk to Tracy."

Tracy jumped when she heard the door to Jon's side of the car open. She relaxed almost immediately when he slid behind the wheel. "Did you get him?"

"No." He turned in the seat and took her hands in his, his eyes searching her face. "Are you all right?"

She nodded, holding on tighter than she would have an hour before. "I've been better but I'll survive. What happens now?" she asked, to give herself something to think about.

"We take you home and, when you feel up to it, we go over what he said to you and what you replied."

"I feel up to it now." She managed a smile. "I didn't realize how unnerving violence could be up close."

"Not like the books at all, is it?"

"That's it in a nutshell. I would flunk the heroine test with my reactions tonight."

Jon didn't let her see that every word she spoke was another whip across his conscience. She had been brave, frightened, but she was still hanging in there. He saw how she was pulling herself together to do what had to be done. Her reactions were normal and understandable. But ultimately they would be more than she could cope with.

He brought her hands to his lips, stifling the need to hold her. Each time she was in his arms, the tie between them grew stronger. He had already paid more than he could afford. For one shining moment he had almost believed they could beat the odds.

Tracy felt something change. The weary, resigned and lost look in Jon's eyes wasn't new. She wanted to demand answers but didn't. Instead she damned the man who had come out of the shadows and touched her with violence. She damned herself for not being hard enough to shake off the light brush with danger and move on as though nothing out of the ordinary had happened. She damned Jon's career for making violence and its effects so important and she damned her own ability to understand just what he was thinking. They were living on borrowed time. Pain was just around the corner. A week. A month. A year. The time span didn't matter. The end did.

"So, where do we start? Do you ask questions or do you want me to just tell you what happened?" She slipped her hands from his, working on a smile.

Jon turned from her smile, missing the way it withered at the edges. "Just go over what happened. I'll take it from there." He didn't want to spook her any more than she already was. Aside from the personal consideration, he needed her information. Starting the car, he guided it away from the fire.

Tracy leaned back in the seat and closed her eyes. Jon would need as clear a picture as she could provide. She had failed them both by letting him see her reaction, but she wouldn't fail him now. Slowly, making sure she missed no detail, no matter how small, she recounted the conversation and described what she'd seen in her brief glimpse of the firebug. She also gave Jon an analysis of Bo's voice. Jon said nothing through the recital.

"Just how long did he talk to you?" Jon asked at the end of the account.

"Maybe a minute and a half."

His brows rose at the information. "You got all of that in ninety seconds? We've got cops on the force that couldn't do as well. Where did you learn to be so observant?"

"Habit. In my business I have to do a lot of sizing people up. It isn't a hard technique to learn."

"But you aren't frightened when you do it as part of your job."

Tracy opened her lips to defend herself, then thought she'd better attack the real source of the problem. "Fear isn't always a detriment. Sometimes it can sharpen your senses, help you do things that would have been out of your range before. I'm surprised you don't remember that instead of giving in to your very biased viewpoint. Don't condemn me because I don't have the same ability or experience in confronting a potentially hazardous situation as you do. You would probably feel an adrenaline rush if I asked you to handle a radio interview without having anyone show you the ropes or sit with you while you face a mike and an unknown audience of thousands."

"I think you handled yourself extremely well. I don't know many people who would have had the nerve to drag the conversation out the way you did once you realized who Bo was," he objected, annoyed at her interpretation.

"That's not the point. Do you think that I don't feel you looking at our future and deciding it doesn't exist?"

Jon stared at the almost empty road, neither denying or agreeing to her words. "All I promised was that I would try. You said it would be enough. Are you changing your mind?"

"You know I'm not. I love you," she said sadly, realizing something that hadn't occurred to her before. "But the love has to be deep enough to make the past seem a dream, not a reality yet unborn."

He turned his head, his eyes holding her for a heartbeat. "Meaning?" he demanded harshly.

"You keep holding on to Amanda but not to me. I'm fighting a ghost. Because she caved in, you think I will, too. Because you never let yourself be free of what you think is your responsibility for her fear, you won't believe I can handle your work. You don't see that she made her choices, but that you both lived with the misery those choices brought her. That was her fault, not yours." The words were so soft they were hard for even her to hear.

She searched his face, seeing more than she wanted. "How do I prove to you that I can face your job? Do something violent? Get kidnapped and come up smiling without a nightmare in sight?"

"Don't be a fool," he replied angrily, his words prodding his temper.

"Then tell me what to do."

Her eyes burned him with her demand for an answer. He swore hard, jerking his gaze back to the road. "You can't *do* anything. Either it works or it doesn't."

"I don't believe in leaving my fate in the lap of the gods. I work for what I get. I earn my place. Tell me how to prove I'm worthy of your love. Tell me how to show you that you can trust me. Give me a direction, a job."

"Damn it, don't put words in my mouth." He turned into her drive with a savage flick of his wrist and then cut the engine before shifting in his seat to face her. "I never asked you to do this. Before you, I've never cared enough about any woman but Amanda to want her in my life. I told you that." He grabbed her shoulders, wanting to shake her hard and yet wanting to crush her in his arms and seal her mouth with his so she could not torture either of them with her words.

Tracy faced him, weary of fighting him. She had thought she could fight anything. She was learning differently. "You come so far and then turn away from me. I tried to understand. I tried to live with the way you push me away. I can't anymore. I've given you all there is in me to give and it isn't enough. I quit. I give up. You win. But know this, it wasn't your work that defeated me. It was you."

She pulled out of his grasp, hating the need to turn away from him. She had believed in him and their future. Once more she had trusted and been betrayed.

"You're tearing us up for no reason." Jon struggled to find a way to reach her.

She ignored him as if he hadn't spoken. "I suppose you still have to be my guard dog. You can sleep in the guest room until this mess is over." She neither looked at him nor acknowledged the harsh indrawn breath that told of his diminishing control. She was too numb to care tonight. Tomorrow the pain would win. But for now, she was safe.

Jon touched her cheek, finding it cold beneath his fingers. "You don't mean that."

"I'm tired. I'm going in." She reached for the door handle, surprised to see how steady her hand was.

Jon frowned at the listless quality in her voice. He caught her chin, turning her head so he could see her eyes. He bit back a curse at the emptiness staring back at him. She wasn't there. If she had not breathed, he would have thought her a statue. She looked through him, showing no emotion even when his fingers slipped down her throat to lightly trace the fullness above her bra.

"I won't be any good tonight. Wait until tomorrow."

Her statement, delivered in a flat monotone, was like an ice-cold shower. His caress stilled.

She smiled faintly at the stunned look on his face. "You thought I would refuse you. I won't. You want a woman who doesn't demand, who is content to benefit from your sexual expertise. So be it. Just wait until poor little me gets over her fright."

She reached up, lifted his hand from her body, dropping it in his lap. This time he made no move to stop her from getting out of the car. He was still sitting where she left him when she opened the house door and then closed it behind her. It was only after her shower when she was sliding into bed that she heard the door open then close again. He was in her home, but she knew he would not come to her, that there would be no warmth and loving between them this night or, perhaps, ever again.

Chapter 14

Jon rolled over, cursing silently. Since this case started he had spent too much time in the wrong bed, cursing his past, cursing his inability to sleep and thinking about decisions he had thought written in stone. Like Tracy he was tired, tired of thinking, worrying and wandering around in confusion as though he didn't have the sense God gave a jackass. It was time he made up his mind. He had the facts. Unless he got off his duff he was going to lose the one woman in the world who meant more to him than any other. It was that simple.

Tracy went downstairs without pausing at the closed door of the guest room. She had nothing left to say. The decision was Jon's now. She knew what she wanted. She was taking a risk, but she believed with all her heart that they could have forever. Jon had the memories of the death of the woman he'd loved and the child she'd almost given him. Tracy couldn't blame him for his fears. That was the horror of it for her—she couldn't really be angry with the stance he had taken. She understood too well. Railing against the fates was equally unproductive. All that was left was getting on with her life as best she could, starting today.

Tracy didn't want breakfast but she was going to eat it. Then she was going into the yard to exhaust herself making a home out of her white elephant.

That was where Jon found her when he finally came down an hour later. He stood in the kitchen doorway and watched her plant small seedlings in one of the flowerbeds they had prepared yesterday. The sun shone in her hair, painting delicate streaks of gold through the rich brown. She was wearing a brief halter top and cutoffs. Her legs were long, tanned and sleek, reaching up to the enticing curve of her bottom. With her back to him he could look his fill without her realizing he was there.

Her hands were gentle as she carefully lifted each seedling from its tiny plastic cup and tucked it into the ground. She worked smoothly, gracefully. With every motion her body dipped and swayed, building an ache deep inside his soul. How could he give up the right to hold her in the night, to make love to her, to be with her when she smiled, to touch her when she needed his strength and to match his mind against hers? Every nerve in him told him to take a chance, but logic screamed no. He had survived the loss of Amanda and even of his child. He would not make it if he lost Tracy.

Tracy knew he was there. She could almost feel the battle taking place within him, but she didn't turn. She didn't want to see his decision until there was no way to put off the moment.

"Look at me," he commanded, coming to stand beside her.

"Why? So that you can tell me I was wrong?"

"No. So I can tell you you were right." He got down on his knees beside her.

She looked into his eyes. Hope flickered brightly in her heart. "You mean it?" She peeled off her gloves.

He winced at the happiness blazing out of her eyes. "I'm afraid and I'm not strong enough to take the risk." He bit the words out, hating the sound, wishing he could make this easier on both of them. "I can't live with what could happen."

From the mountain of hope to the pit of the despair in one plummet. She hit ground so hard that there wasn't air to breathe, much less to fight.

"I can't leave you until this is over. But I won't touch you, and that's going to be the hardest thing I've ever done in my life." His hands curled into fists as he watched her crumble before his eyes.

"It's that easy for you," she whispered, not having accepted until this moment that he really could walk out of her life.

"No." Jon hurt in ways he didn't know existed. He wanted to take back every word but couldn't. He wanted to hold her in his arms and whisper all the promises she deserved. But he did nothing. Every muscle strained at the effort to face her. "I thought losing Amanda was an impossible price. I was wrong."

She closed her eyes against the terrible truth he offered her. Without the words he was telling her that he cared more for her than Amanda. Gathering every ounce of strength left in her body, she forced herself to look at him. "Then it's over."

"When I know you're safe, I'll go." He inhaled deeply, wondering when the pain would stop.

Tracy glanced down at her plants. "I need to get these in the ground. I'll leave you to do whatever you wish to amuse yourself." She pulled on her gloves. One foot ahead of the other, she reminded herself silently. She had survived Lee, betrayal and uprooting her life to begin with. She would survive this. She always survived, despite what Jon thought.

"You look like death warmed over, buddy," Roger said, glancing up as Jon sat down at his desk.

Jon opened a file folder, knowing Roger was telling the truth. The past five days had been sheer torture. He hadn't realized what being with Tracy without having her would mean to him. True to his word he had stayed in the guest room at night. The past two nights he'd retired to it at the earliest possible moment after dinner. Tracy had been quiet but not silent, going about her routine as though he were someone she barely knew. She cooked dinner, he handled breakfast. She worked in the house or the yard every night after work, neither refusing his help nor demanding it.

They discussed the case and the absence of phone calls from the firebug. She looked at Jon without seeing him, and he tried to tell himself that the distance between them was for the best. It wasn't working. His temper was suffering, his sleep was intermittent and his appetite almost non-existent. He felt drawn on a rack with no hope of escape. But worst of all was the knowledge that it was his own hand that turned the wheel of torture.

"I feel like hell," he admitted at length. He looked up, needing to talk.

Roger frowned, studying him. "You picked a stupid time to change your mind about how you want to live your life. I never thought your interest in Tracy was anything more than admiration, and maybe later a case of good old-fashioned lust for a sexy lady."

Jon ignored the last comment to focus on the more important first part. "I haven't changed it, that's just the problem."

Roger's eyes widened as the information sifted through. He whistled softly. "With the way you feel about commitment and the lengths you go to avoid it, even in the few friendships you allow yourself, I can see what you mean. What are you going to do?"

"I'm getting out just as soon as this mess is cleared up."

Roger frowned skeptically. "If it's that easy for you why do you look like walking death?"

Jon shrugged, his irritation plain. "I didn't say it was easy." He glanced around the busy room, wishing he hadn't started the discussion. No one was paying them the slightest attention but he had no idea how long that would last. "Just forget I said anything. It's my problem. I'll solve it."

"Not that way, you won't." Roger sighed deeply. "I've worked with you and practically lived in your pocket for almost eight years. I've seen you make decisions that I wouldn't have had the nerve to attempt. I watched you after Amanda. And through it all I've never once seen you run from anything—until now. Believe me, if you're in love, running won't help."

Jon was in no mood to hear any advice from love-'em-and-leave-'em Roger. The sarcasm erupted before he knew it. "What would you know about love?"

Roger's lips twisted, his eyes dark with memories that only a blind man would have missed. "You'd be surprised. But it isn't my life on the block. Tell yourself you can take a hike. Try it, too, if you want, but it won't matter in the end. You'll close your eyes to reality and give it a shot."

"You're nuts. If I back down, it won't be just me that's hurt. It'll be Tracy," Jon muttered.

"So you're telling yourself it's better to hurt her now than later. Smart move, buddy. Not only do you squelch your own life but hers too. Looks to me like the lady should have the right to make her own choices about what she can take and what she can't. Of course, you know her better than I do." Roger shook his head, smiling grimly. "Just don't say I didn't warn you. I didn't get the way I am on my own. And I also didn't reach thirty-five without making more mistakes than I intend to remember."

Having said his piece, he picked up the list of employee matches he had been working on and passed it to Jon. "Take a look at that and see if it doesn't get your mind off your personal life for a minute."

Jon had never felt less like dealing with his work or the puzzles that usually intrigued him to the exclusion of all else. Only professional pride and gut-level determination made him concentrate on the computer printouts. "You were right about the social security numbers. It took a while, but the computer finally managed to unscramble the digits to come up with a one-number and one-name match for Bo. It was Bob Little. But we also came up with something odd in the long background check the other team was doing. There's another man, Ron Little. Same last name as Bo. Out of the businesses burned, Ronny worked in almost every place that Bo did, all within the past five years. It's like Bo is deliberately following Ron's employment record right down the coast. We've got the police checking now in the small town in Virginia where the social security records say both men were born. Another funny thing is both were born on the same day.''

"Twins?"

Roger nodded. "Looks that way. But more than that—the second brother is dead. Killed himself with an overdose of pills and booze right here in town."

"Bo said something to Tracy about justice and paying. But for what? How do the jobs connect with Ron's suicide?"

"There was nothing in the information from the companies hit about a major problem with any of the employees," Roger commented.

"Dig deeper. There must be someone in those businesses who remembers Ron. Find out what he was like, what kind of problems he might have had or caused. Use your charm or whatever it takes but get it today. Also see if you can find out the last place Ron worked. If we can, we might just be able to stop Bo and prevent one last fire."

Jon folded the papers and tucked them into his pocket. "If you need me I'll be at the radio station. I think I'll have a talk with Tracy."

Tracy finished the notes she was making on her discussion with a local school board member. The woman would be guesting on her show next week to rebut the recent criticism leveled at the board for changing the school district boundaries. The phone rang. Tracy picked it up, her mind on the upcoming show rather than the caller. But the sound of Bo's voice on the other end snagged her attention in an instant.

"Bo?"

"I want to see you tonight. I want you to understand."

"Understand what?" She had to keep him talking, she reminded herself, as she cursed the fact that the room was empty and there was no way to signal anyone what was going on. There was the trace on this phone and the one at home, but Jon had wanted her to alert someone when the calls took place just to be on the safe side.

"Why I set the fires," he said impatiently. He gripped the list of directions he had printed on the paper in front of him. He hadn't wanted to forget anything. "I want you to meet me at the old Kaiser Building on Fourteenth Street. I'll be in the back parking lot. Come alone. No Kent. Twelve tonight."

"That area isn't safe at that hour," she objected, trying to keep the conversation going.

"I'll be there. I didn't let that glass get to you that night, did I? I won't let anything happen to you. I promise."

Disturbed by the gentle, almost tender, note in his voice, Tracy wasn't quick enough with a comment to hold his attention. He hung up, disconnecting them before the time had elapsed to allow a successful trace. Disturbed, discouraged and worried, she propped her elbows on the desk and tried to think clearly. She had no doubt Jon would have an alternative plan, but she doubted that the firebug would accept any substitutes. That left only her to carry out instructions, which meant she would have to convince Jon to let her take the risk. For that little achievement she hadn't a clue as to how to begin.

Bo leaned his head against the cold Formica on the tabletop and tried to slow his breathing. Sweat stood out in drops on his face and dampened his T-shirt. So close. One more fire, ironically the biggest building of them all. Ron would have been proud of him. By this time tomorrow everyone would know how Ron had died and why. And Bo would be able to stop running, to cease looking over his shoulder. There would be peace in his life once more, he'd have brought justice to those who had driven Ron to his death.

Heartened by the thought, he took a deep breath and lifted his head. The gas and diesel mixture that would start the fire stood in large plastic containers in the corner. The eight timers were already made and stored in his backpack. The small explosives he had created out of common household items were sitting innocently on the table in front of him. He was ready. He had the timing set to the last second. He would meet Tracy, explain and then leave her in order to plant his fire bombs in his last target. He would have twenty minutes, including a margin of error of a minute and a half, to make it out of the building before the first bomb went off. There would be four minutes between the first and last explosions. Once the hole was blown in the roof, nothing would stop his orange beast from devouring its last victim. He smiled at the thought, wishing Ron could have lived to share the victory with him.

Tracy fielded the next call, trying to concentrate on her show. Where was Jon? When she phoned him he'd said he'd be right over. There hadn't been time to go into detail then about Bo's demand for a meeting. She shifted restlessly while probing her listener for information. Suddenly a movement in the control room caught her eye. The sight of Jon's reassuring bulk stilled her restlessness almost immediately. The tension in her muscles fled and it was all she could do not to sigh deeply over the mike. His eyes held hers as he took a chair beside Nikki. She glanced at the clock on the wall. Ten minutes until the news break in the middle of her two-hour show. The long hand crawled around the clock as she dealt with the lottery debate.

"How about watching the board for me while the phone lines are filled?" the director asked Nikki. "I need to talk to the boss for a sec." He rose from his stool and slipped out of the small room as soon as she nodded her agreement.

"What have you been doing to her?" Nikki demanded of Jon in a harsh whisper as soon as they were alone.

Jon looked at Tracy's friend. Keeping his face blank took effort. Until this morning he hadn't realized how Tracy was affected by the strain between them. He had been so wrapped up in his own emotions he hadn't seen the faint circles of sleeplessness under her eyes, the gentle hollows beneath her cheekbones that told of a recent weight loss. Even her hair seemed to have lost some of its luster.

"Although now that I look at you, you must be doing a number on yourself, too," Nikki added when Jon didn't answer immediately. "You look terrible."

"I feel it," Jon surprised himself by admitting.

"I thought you two had something going."

"We did up to a point."

Nikki frowned. "What does that mean?" She shook her head. "No, scratch that. It's your business and Tracy's. But let me tell you this, big guy, she is a heck of a woman. You treat her right or I'll find a way to make your life more miserable than it already looks like it is."

Jon grimaced at the vehemence in Nikki's voice but made no comment. He had no defense.

The warning beep for the national news break sounded, bringing an end to the silence in the control room. Nikki cued Tracy as Jon rose from his chair. Tracy pulled off the headphones and got to her feet. Jon met her at the door, his eyes searching hers.

"What's up?"

"Bo wants me to meet him at midnight tonight. He's ready to tell us why he's setting the fires."

"Finally! A break we can get our teeth into. But he sure didn't give us much time to set up a double for you."

"I don't want a double. He said he wanted to see me alone and I'm going." She braced herself for Jon's objections. She didn't have long to wait.

"Over my dead body."

Chapter 15

It's the only way," Tracy argued.

Jon was determined to make her listen to reason. "You don't know what you're talking about. I don't tell you how to run your show, so don't tell me how to set a scene like this. Meeting Bo is dangerous. We still don't have a complete handle on his motive. And you aren't trained to take risks. For all you know he could want a hostage and has been setting you up. No way are you going in there alone."

Tracy glared at him, ignoring the scenery flashing by the car as Jon drove them home. "We've been arguing about this all day. I listened to that psychologist, your boss, my boss and even your partner, and not one of you has come up with a foolproof way to pull off this meeting without me. It would be different if he didn't know what I look like. But he does so there's no way he's going to be fooled by any double. He's also shown that he's very cautious. If I don't go you lose whatever chance you have of catching him."

"It's not worth the risk to you," he said flatly.

Tracy bit her lip to keep back the hot words aching for expression. "You can't keep protecting me. That's what I've been trying to tell you. I have a right to make my own choices, take my own risks. I don't ask you not to go out on the streets and make yourself a target. I'm no glory hound nor do I have any death wish. I'm scared, and if you could show me any way that putting someone in my place would serve as well, I'd bow out without a whimper. But you can't and you know it."

Jon turned into her drive and stopped the car. "You don't know how bad it could get."

"No, I don't, and I hope to heaven I don't find out," she added with great feeling. "But I'm going to do this. There's simply no other way. You can't talk me out of doing what I can. Even your boss and mine agreed it's the only way. You and Roger and the six-man team you intend to have hovering around the area should ensure my safety. I'll wear a wire. I'll be all right." She met his eyes without flinching. So much more than just catching the firebug hinged on Jon's ability to let the past die. She wouldn't have chosen this way to make her point, but now that the opportunity presented itself, she couldn't deny herself one last shot at making him see reason.

"Tell them you've changed your mind." Jon reached for her, unable to bear the thought of her in danger. "Back out of this and marry me." The words emerged out of need rather than intent.

Tracy stiffened in his arms, feeling the tears sting her eyes. "Marriage isn't a sugar pill or a bribe." She looked at him, seeing his fear and the past that haunted him still. "Let me go, Jon." She felt his resistance, the desire riding him. Her body knew its mate but it still wasn't enough.

"Damn you." He pushed her away to run his fingers through his hair. "Don't ask me to do this."

"I'm not asking you to do anything." His torment was hers. She wanted to hold him, to give them both peace. "I love you, Jon, but I wouldn't have used my love to ask you to go against what you believe is right." She opened the car door and stepped into the night. "You said you cared about me. If that's true, how could *you* ask that of *me*?" Without waiting for an answer, she headed for the house, leaving Jon to follow or not as he chose.

She wanted to cry but didn't. The hurt was too deep and she still had to get through the meeting that had torn them even farther apart. Going upstairs, she showered and changed into jeans and the light-colored shirt specified by the police. They wanted to be able to spot her easily.

All that was left to be done was to attach the microphone just before she switched from Jon's car to her own for the short drive from the radio station where it had been parked to the rendezvous point.

Jon was waiting for her when she went downstairs. He said nothing, although she could feel his eyes following her as she headed for the kitchen.

"I'm going to fix myself some supper. Do you want some?" She wasn't hungry, but she needed food to provide the energy to make it through the next few hours. Plus making dinner gave her something to do besides waiting and brooding.

"Tell me what to do and I'll help."

Tracy didn't look at him as he spoke. "No. I'd rather do it alone."

Jon came to her, unable to bear the distance and the coldness between them. "I wish I had met you first."

She turned to him then. "Well, I don't. You are who you are because of your experiences, just as I am. I love you now. I want you flaws and all."

"You said no to marrying me," he reminded her.

"I said no to the *price* of marrying you," she corrected starkly.

He stared at her, suddenly deciding the cost of what he was doing to them was too high. She was right about the meet, and it was time he admitted it. "All right. I'll go along with this setup, but I don't like it."

She hadn't expected even that much of a concession. She understood the effort it took for him to bend so much. Controlling the tears of pain had been difficult, but stopping the tears of relief was impossible. "You mean it?"

He drew her into his arms, finding a measure of peace at last. "I worry. I can't help it. I held you after that phone call and saw what it did to you." He leaned his head against her hair and savored the feel of her in his arms. The light teasing of her scent was more familiar than home.

"I told you before, I'm a survivor. I don't know how to be anything else. Just trust me." She turned to look him in the eye.

"I'm trying," he said with a deep sigh. His arms tightened around her. "Against every instinct I have, I'm trying."

"That's all I ask." She went up on her tiptoes to brush his lips with hers. At the first touch, he hungrily took all that she offered and more. Tracy leaned into the kiss, as desperate for him as he seemed to be for her. She didn't know what the future held. But at least for now, they were together—and there was hope. But Jon's demons were alive, real and strong. And she had no weapons with which to fight but her love.

Bo stared down the road that would bring her to him. Anticipation heated his blood. Even his first fire hadn't given him the same feeling of lightness that this meeting with Tracy offered. He had watched her for so long. Now he would see her again, be near her, and she would know him. It wouldn't be like the other time when he had had to run away and leave her. They would talk. She would understand. She would tell him he had done as he should, She would mourn Ron just as he did. She would help him make the world see how cruel it was.

Light flashed in the darkness. He tensed. Tracy had arrived. The car stopped. He recognized it. She was alone. He trembled with eagerness.

"I'm here, Jon." Tracy spoke softly into the microphone Jon had taped close to her right breast. "I don't see anything as yet. It's not surprising because it's dark as the inside of a tomb. I take that back. Leave out the tomb part."

Jon frowned when he heard the nervous sigh coming from Tracy's end of the mike. "Damn, I hate this. Can't we get any closer?"

Roger gripped the steering wheel, his eyes straining at the darkness. "You know we can't. The Kaiser Building is just too isolated from the rest of the offices. If the firebug is anywhere near the top he has too good a view of us. Just take it easy, buddy. We've got the place surrounded. Your lady will be all right. And she's got her head on straight. Maybe she's a tad nervous, but she's doing fine.''

"I still don't like this." Jon stared at the spot too many yards away. He could just make out Tracy's car. He tensed as he saw a shadow move close to the vehicle. "There he is." He punched the mike that connected him with each of the other teams. "Look alive guys, it's going down."

Tracy scanned the area while still trying to look as if midnight meetings were an everyday occurrence for her. Jon had stressed how important it was to stay calm. None of them wanted to spook Bo. She breathed deeply, wishing she dared talk to Jon through the mike again. Anything would have been better than waiting silently like a lamb staked out for a marauding tiger. Mentally cursing the morbid images that seemed to be filling her mind, she shifted in her seat, almost jumping out of the car when Bo spoke close to her left shoulder.

"It's me. It's all right. You don't have to be afraid."

Tracy stared at the slight figure dressed completely in black. She wasn't afraid. What she felt was closer to restrained panic.

"Bo?" She queried hesitantly, remembering to use words to let her backup know what was going on.

He smiled at her, wanting her to relax. "You must be hot in the car. Come out here. There's a breeze." He stepped back, raising his hands so that she could see they were empty. "I won't hurt you. I only want to talk, and then you can go."

She pictured Jon's warning in mile-high letters: DON'T GET OUT OF THE CAR. She looked at Bo, saw that he expected her to leave her sanctuary. If she didn't do as he said, she might make him suspicious. She was torn between not making him nervous and protecting herself.

"Tracy, please. I promise, I won't lay a finger on you."

The determined plea was too strong to ignore. Tracy unlocked the door and slipped from the car. Yards away, six men cursed, but held their positions.

"You can close the car door and come with me."

Tracy shook her head. "I think I'll stay here. You wanted to talk to me and you were right. It is cooler out here than in the car. But I don't really know you." Since he seemed to be trying to reassure her, Tracy decided to take a chance on appealing to his protective attitude.

He studied her, then turned his head to scan the area. "You did come alone, didn't you?"

"You don't see anyone else, do you?"

"No." He smiled again, relaxing. "I wasn't sure you'd come. I thought your cop would stop you, or didn't you tell him you were coming to see me?"

Tracy didn't like the way he had phrased the remark but let it pass. "You told me to come alone. If I had told Jon, he would have come with me. But I must hurry or he'll miss me."

Bo scowled, not liking the reminder. "All right. I promised you the story and this is it." He inhaled deeply and looked away from her face for a moment. Finally he turned back, bracing himself. "Every one of these fires—and there are a lot of them—has to do with my twin brother, Ron. The owners of every one of these businesses hurt him. Not one of them saw how special he was, not ordinary like me. He was brilliant in school and great on the football field. I couldn't play anything well. He was everything I wasn't and more. We were pals, Ron and I.''

He paused, shifting restlessly, remembering his father's bullying, his brother's defense. ''He made life at home bearable, always joking when Dad went on a binge and beat us. Mom had gone long before those days. I loved Ron and I watched him die, because the world didn't see how special he was. He had to quit high school in our junior year to go to work so we could eat. Dad went away that year. Ron wouldn't let me quit school. He said one of us had to have an education. He went to work in Richmond. The salaries were higher there. When I graduated, he tried to go back to school, but the kids ragged him so much he had to stop.''

Rage built in Bo with each memory. ''They just wouldn't let him alone. He got a job at my office, cleaning up while he went to night school. They fired him for sleeping on the job. He got another job. He failed night school that term and lost the job, because he wasn't keeping up with his agreement to finish school. He got another job, with a company that didn't care about his schooling, but it didn't pay as much. From then on the jobs got worse, the bosses harder. Ron couldn't face his life. He drank, hating himself. He tried to dry out and pick up his life again. But everyone saw only his employment record, not the real man. No boss would give him a chance. He drifted south, always looking, always trying to put the pieces back together again.'' Bo paused, trying to control the need to hit out at something. He had to finish his story.

"Ron ended up here in West Palm Beach, drinking, hurting and alone. He called me the night he turned forty. He was drinking and had taken a bottle of pills as well, but I didn't know it. He was crying." Tears stood in Bo's eyes as he recalled the scene. "I loved him but I couldn't save him. I couldn't make his life clean and new again. But I could make those who cut him up into little pieces pay. And I have. I want justice."

Tracy felt like crying herself, but she made sure she didn't show it. Instead she asked the one question plaguing her. "Where did you learn to handle fires this way?"

Bo laughed harshly. "The first one was an accident, and it gave me the idea. After that I went to the library. Great places, libraries. You can find all kinds of information there, and if they don't have it they'll send off to people who do—even if you're investigating how to make fire bombs."

Tracy read the pain and disillusionment in Bo's eyes, knowing he spoke the truth and that he had come too far to turn away from the completion of his goal. "What do you want me to do specifically?"

"I want you to make sure that the real truth gets out. I don't trust the newspapers. Nothing can help Ron or me now. I've escaped the police for a long time. Your friend Kent has a rep on the street for always getting his man. I knew I'd get caught when I started this, but I don't care. Ron was worth it." He stepped closer, wanting to touch her just for a moment. He lifted his hand.

In the distance Jon froze, listening to and watching the scene. Bo's confession had touched Tracy. Jon heard the compassion in her voice. He could feel Bo's

need to make his peace, perhaps a final peace. The
man had almost finished what he started out to do. He
had nothing to look forward to but a jail sentence.
And Tracy was in the middle, caught between a person with nothing more to lose and a system that intended to stop him. Jon thumbed the talk button on
the mike. "Everyone hold your positions," he bit out
tersely.

A second later, the sound of a cough and a curse
rent the night. In an instant the scene broke into a
mass of action and voices.

At the sound Bo turned, crouching low. "It was a
trap," he said to Tracy angrily. His eyes were glitter-
ing with betrayal and frustration.

Tracy jumped into the car, trying to shut and lock
the door. Bo caught her arm, jerking her out of the car
toward him. At the same moment, Roger put his vehicle in motion while Jon gave the command to close
the net.

"Let's go." Bo dragged Tracy into the shadows.

Tracy fought the grip on her arm but Bo was
stronger than he looked. Stumbling, she trailed him,
making him drag her weight as much as she could. He
hardly seemed to notice as he led her into an alley that
was too narrow for cars. She could hear the shouts of
her backup. Her breath was coming in short pants as
she and Bo suddenly veered to the right. A second later
she was shoved into a car, and they were speeding
through the almost deserted streets. Realizing Jon
might be lost, Tracy tried to pay attention to their
route.

"Why are we heading south on U.S.1? Where are
you taking me?" She didn't have to pretend to be a
frightened woman babbling out questions in order to

give the men listening to her hidden mike directions. At the moment she wasn't sure she'd ever be calm again.

"Shut up. Your boyfriend won't find you."

"Be careful! You're going to send us into the lake if you take the turn so fast. Thank God we're next to the hospital."

"I said shut up." Bo gave her a savage look. "One more word out of you and I'll hit you."

Tracy shut up for the instant it took to take a deep breath. Being hit was better than being lost from her backup. At least with them close behind she had a chance. "I can't help it. I don't understand any of this. You're doubling back on yourself."

Bo swore and took the curving road at high speed. "I'm giving you a ringside seat to the last job." He made two more turns and pulled into a deserted parking lot next to a seven-story office complex.

"Boyer Associates," Tracy said.

Bo didn't answer. He reached in the back seat and yanked the knapsack into his lap. He had trusted her. She had betrayed him. He was torn between wanting to hurt her the way she had hurt him and the need to ensure her safety. "See this? It has enough stuff in it to make a number of big bangs. Now you be good and you might make it through this night. Don't run, don't try to get away and don't jar me. Understand?"

Tracy nodded. She had done her best to give Jon directions. The rest was up to him.

"Then let's go." Bo got out of the car and gestured for her to slide across the seat to get out on his side. "I'll be one step behind you. If by some miracle your lover finds us, none of us will walk away. Now get going."

Tracy accepted Bo's directions without question. She wasn't even sure Jon had heard her clues, because the range for the mike she wore was short. She had to believe he did. She had to trust his ability and his strength. If there were a way to reach her, Jon would find it.

"Stop here." Bo slipped off the knapsack and took out one of the timers. He handed Tracy the pack. "Now if you're very careful, nothing will happen."

Tracy felt the rough fabric in her hands. She looked at the innocent bag with a sense of horror. Bo had found the perfect way to ensure her staying in one place. She wouldn't have moved if God himself told her to. They set the rest of the charges on various floors with the same procedure.

At last she and Bo were on the roof, the last charge set. With each moment that passed, Tracy grew more worried, felt more alone. Jon was her lifeline. She needed him as she never had before. And then Jon was there.

"That's it, Bo."

Bo turned, his eyes narrowing to slits. "So the cop finds us at last." He caught hold of Tracy's arm, dragging her closer as he yanked a knife from a small sheath on his hip. He laid the blade against Tracy's throat. "You don't want to hold us up. The timers are set with just enough time for me to get out of the building."

"You're not going anywhere." Jon took a step nearer, his gun drawn. He had no backup. Every member of the team was busy with the fire people and the bomb squad trying to find the charges. With Tracy on the roof they didn't dare let the fire start. "You don't have any place to go. My men are downstairs disarming the timers now."

Bo smiled, his face twisted with hate. "It doesn't matter. This one here will do the trick. I don't want to hurt anyone but you leave me no choice. Maybe it's even better this way. I didn't want to stand trial."

Tracy stared at Jon, willing him to find a way out for them all. He was so calm, so at ease, while she felt as if she was shaking into a hundred pieces.

Jon knew he didn't have much time. He had to distract Bo and get that knife, but he was too far away. "You die up here with her, and no one's going to sympathize with you or your brother. You'll be just another dirty little man hitting out at people more successful than you or your twin. Is that what you want? Ron's death won't be vindicated. The guilty won't know they've been punished." Jon didn't allow his gaze to stray to Tracy as he pushed Bo, hoping to make him angry enough to turn the knife in his direction instead of Tracy's. "You don't want to hurt Tracy. We made her help us. She didn't want to. She cares about you and your brother." He inched closer. One more step and he would be within striking distance of Bo. He had to get that knife away from Tracy's throat. He had to get her off the roof and to safety.

"You're lying. She led you to me. I trusted her."

"She didn't want to. I lied to her to get her help. We wired her. My men and I heard the whole story, but she's the only one who'll tell it the way you want. But she can't if she dies up here. So let her go." Another inch. He tensed. All he needed now was an opening.

Tracy had seen Jon's maneuvering. At first she hadn't understood his actions, then suddenly she knew what he intended. With every step he took, she shifted her weight slightly, throwing more of it back on her heels. She would be taking a chance, but it was the only one either she or Jon had. Jon wouldn't make a move as long as the knife was at her throat. She had to distract Bo without getting cut. Drawing a deep breath, she sent up a silent prayer as she leaned back, turned and dropped in a jerky little motion that threw Bo off balance.

Jon jumped him, shoving her out of the way. "Run. Get out of here. Now," he commanded roughly.

The knife went flying but then so did Jon's gun. Ignoring the orders, Tracy scrambled on her hands and knees to escape the slamming together of two male bodies. The tangle of arms and legs, the grunts and thuds of violence expended was an obscene sound in the still of the night.

She hardly noticed. Her whole attention was trained on finding Jon's gun. She had heard that madmen often fought with the strength of ten, and she didn't want Jon hurt. Finally her fingers found the cold metal. She got shakily to her feet, focusing on the fight. Bo and Jon were locked in an bone-crushing embrace. She couldn't get a clear bead on Bo. Circling, swearing at her own ineptitude, she almost stumbled over the last charge. A horrified glance at the clock face revealed that there were only two minutes to go. The elevator ride down took almost that long.

Suddenly, she took a desperate chance. Holding the gun skyward in both hands, she pulled the trigger. The shock made Bo freeze long enough for Jon to get in a Sunday punch. Bo went down without a whimper.

"We have about one minute, Jon," she said, running to him.

Jon glance at her, saw the fear overshadowed by a kind of desperate courage. He reached down and heaved Bo over his shoulder. "Then let's make tracks." He caught her hand and started for the door leading to the single flight of stairs that ended at the elevator.

Tracy matched him step for step. The elevator soon became crowded as each member of the team got on for the final ride to the ground. Jon still held Tracy's hand as they raced for the front doors and safety. The group cleared the building just as the explosion hit. The fire crew rushed into the building before the echo of the detonation had a chance to die. Jon turned his prisoner over to Roger without looking at the unconscious man.

Pulling the gun out of Tracy's hand, he placed it in his holster and then yanked her in his arms. His kiss was hard and deep, a punishment and a man's celebration of success. Tracy gave herself to the primitive possession, feeling a need to do a little celebrating of her own.

Jon came up for air, glaring down at her. "You fool. You could have been killed for taking a chance like that. That damn knife was at your throat. As for that stunt with the gun—this isn't a Western movie."

Tracy glared right back at him. "And what was I supposed to do? Leave you up there with that lunatic to get yourself blown to pieces? In a pig's eye. I saw you moving in. If I hadn't flopped around like a dying fish you wouldn't have been able to jump him. As for the gun—I don't know how to shoot. If I'd taken aim at Bo I probably would have hit you." She planted her hands on her hips, so angry she could barely talk. Half of Jon's team was standing by as an audience. She

didn't care. She had had enough of being understanding and being wrapped up like a lovely doll,
protected from life.

"And another thing. I've decided to change my
mind. I think I will marry you. You need a keeper."

Incensed, Jon stared at her as though she had left
her brains on the roof. "*I* need a keeper?" he roared,
also oblivious to the crowd of onlookers. "I told you
to stay in that car."

"If I had, that turkey would have run and you know
it. Just be thankful I watch enough TV so that I knew
how to let you know where I was."

"She's got you there, Jon," Roger inserted, crossing his arms over his chest while enjoying the show.
"All in all I think she did a super job."

Jon stared at his woman, listening to her blaze at
him, suddenly knowing he had almost made the biggest mistake of his life. He loved Tracy and she could
handle anything. She might have been scared but she
hadn't run. She might have taken some chances but
they hadn't been foolish ones. In short, had she been
anyone else he would have been grateful for her help.
Tracy wasn't Amanda. The future didn't come with a
guarantee. The present was all that mattered. He
opened his mouth to tell her but didn't get the chance
to speak.

Tracy didn't need any help. "Roger, you shut up.
One of you almost got us killed. I distinctly heard Jon
tell everyone not to make a move or a sound until we
found out where the next bomb would be." She missed
Roger's openmouthed reaction as well as the sudden
silence of men looking at the culprit and his shame-
faced response as she returned her attention to Jon.

"And another thing. Don't you ever lecture me on being careful. Or being afraid. I think I used up my quota for the year, make that forever." Feeling her legs go weak as reaction began to set in she wobbled to Jon's car and got in. "I want to go home. I'm tired. And I've had enough excitement for one night."

Jon chuckled at the irritated grumble. His lady was winding down.

"Don't laugh at me, you rat. I'm still not happy with you."

He leaned into the car, his lips covering hers before she could start on him again. "I surrender, love. You can stop calling me names and lecturing my friends. I love you and you're right. I do need a keeper, so I'm taking you up on your offer." He kissed her again when her jaw dropped slightly in shock.

Tracy searched his face. "No ghosts?"

He framed her face with his hands, ignoring the smudges of grime on the delicate skin. "Not one. I watched that knife at your throat tonight and knew life wouldn't be worth living without you. I've been a fool and a coward and anything else you'd like to call me to throw away one minute of our love for fear of your being taken from me. I was also a fool for not trusting your love. I want you and everything you want to share with me. I want to give you everything I have and am. For now, forever."

Tracy caught his wrists, feeling his pulse beat beneath her fingers. "I love you. Take us home."

* * * * *

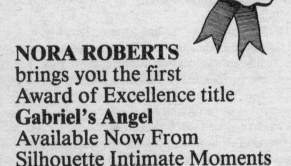

Silhouette Intimate Moments®

NORA ROBERTS
brings you the first
Award of Excellence title
Gabriel's Angel
Available Now From
Silhouette Intimate Moments

They were on a collision course with love....

*Laura Malone was alone, scared—and pregnant. She was running
for the sake of her child. Gabriel Bradley had his own problems.
He had neither the need nor the inclination to get involved in
someone else's.*

*But Laura was like no other woman...and she needed him. Soon
Gabe was willing to risk all for the heaven of her arms.*

The Award of Excellence is given to one specially selected title per
month. Look for the second Award of Excellence title, coming out in
September from Silhouette Romance—**SUTTON'S WAY**
by Diana Palmer

IM 300-1A

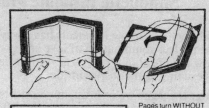

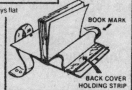

Silhouette Intimate Moments®

COMING IN OCTOBER!
A FRESH LOOK FOR
Silhouette Intimate Moments!

Silhouette Intimate Moments has always brought you the perfect combination of love and excitement, and now they're about to get a new cover design that's just as exciting as the stories inside.

Over the years we've brought you stories that combined romance with something a little bit different, like adventure or suspense. We've brought you longtime favorite authors like Nora Roberts and Linda Howard. We've brought you exciting new talents like Patricia Gardner Evans and Marilyn Pappano. Now let us bring you a new cover design guaranteed to catch your eye just as our heroes and heroines catch your heart.

Look for it in October—
Only from Silhouette Intimate Moments!